DEVIL MOON
OVER PHILADELPHIA

THE OTHER PHILADELPHIA STORY

M. Brown McNally

Fulton Books
Meadville, PA

Published by Fulton Books 2023

Front and Rear Cover design: A collaboration by commercial
artist and illustrator Ulana Zahajkewycz and the author

Library of Congress Registration Number: TXu 2-311-797

ISBN 978-1-63985-686-2 (paperback)
ISBN 978-1-63985-688-6 (hardcover)
ISBN 978-1-63985-687-9 (digital)

Printed in the United States of America

DEDICATION

To Roberta, my beloved wife of forty-six years.
She supported and encouraged me to write this,
my first book, my paternal family's history.

AUTHOR'S INTRODUCTION

This book is a historical novel tracing five generations of my paternal family. It follows a chronological timeline and combines elements of history, facts from research, some mixed with fiction, as well as a touch of myth and legend, to tell the story that begins in 1778 in Glasgow, Scotland. The roots of my family had their beginnings there, where two brave souls fled Scotland and immigrated to Ireland in search of a new and better life.

Why the first McNallys in my family chose to leave Scotland is a mystery, but, invoking the author's privilege, I chose one such possible reason, related to the church practices of the time and how they dealt with unwed mothers. Unwed mothers were chastised in the church for weeks and then sent to asylums. Their children were then sent to orphanages, where they were often abused and sometimes killed. Of those who escaped or left the orphanage as adults, most never found their parents or relatives.

The story beginning in Glasgow in 1778 is a fact. The names of the family members there are real. The family events at that time are possible but fictitious.

Records of my genealogy during the eighteenth century are sketchy at best, as searching the family name back further became fruitless. McNally literally means "son of a poor man." With a plethora of McNallys scattered all over the British Isles and now all over the world, searching for specific family members back further in time was impossible.

The places in the book are real, as are the descriptions of those times and places. The 1700 dates are approximate, as the researched dates varied by a year or so depending on the source.

There are fictional characters, other than my family members, that have been added throughout the book, along with other local characters and events, to weave the story through the history of the times as it might have been. Some actual historic waypoints have been embedded in the story to add a historical timeline perspective.

As the story eventually develops, it focuses on the life of my great-grandfather, Peter David McNally, born in County Armagh, Ireland, in 1834, who grew up on a farm there, lived with his family through the great famine, and in 1847, at the age of sixteen, immigrated first to New York City and eventually moved to Philadelphia.

He married an Irish woman, Bridget Cunningham. The couple had ten children during their marriage. The McNally family suffered many hardships and tragedies—business failures, sickness, and disease, early deaths of children, and the cold-blooded murder of Peter's favorite daughter.

All the places and most of the events in Philadelphia are true. Names of government officials who had a role in the murder story are real, as are the details of the murder trial. Historical and genealogical records for this period of time are excellent and include archival newspapers from the 1800s into the 1900s. Local characters, actual places, and minor events have been added as they were, or likely may have been, in those days.

The actual events that occurred in Philadelphia were researched and chronicled in local Philadelphia newspapers, books about Irish immigration, and the history of Philadelphia at the time—the 1800s through 1910. Other books, libraries, and archival sources were also used and are footnoted.

As with many families, there are oral histories of successes, sorrows, and even tragedies that get handed down from generation to generation. That was not the case with my family. There is often a "skeleton in the closet," an event so heinous, so unthinkable that it was sworn to secrecy, to be taken to the grave, never to be told.

Such was the intent of the McNally family, but this author found the secret.

I was inspired to write this, my first book when building my family tree on ancestry.com in 2016. I made a startling discovery—a one hundred-thirty-two-year-old "skeleton in the closet" was found, and the secret was revealed. That secret is now shared in *Devil Moon over Philadelphia.*

PROLOGUE

Tuesday, January 13, 1778
Smyllum Park Orphanage
Lanark, Lanarkshire, Scotland
10:30 p.m.

"Do you see that Devil Moon out there, child? It's a sign that you are a child of the devil! Do you hear me?" the nun screamed as she continually beat the six-year-old child that she had stripped of her clothing and tied facedown to a bed in the "punishing room." She was being beaten because she was a "crier," a sure sign she was possessed by the devil. The beatings continued alternately with a crucifix and a cane leaving open gashes on the young girl's back, buttocks, and legs. The child's scream of terror echoed, seemingly unnoticed, through the halls of the Orphanage. The orphanage, some ten kilometers southeast of Glasgow, was run by the Daughters of Charity of St. Vincent de Paul.

"Your mother hated you and did not want you! You are evil and must be punished!"

The nun continued while the child kept screaming, "Stop, stop!"

With the might of her two hands gripping the cane held high over the child, she delivered a blow to the back of the child's head. God stopped the torture. The child was dead. She was buried before sunrise in an unmarked grave in the field behind the orphanage with the others. This was an extreme of the abuses at the orphanage yet a part of the norm. Children were physically and sexually abused. Some died. No one at the orphanage cared. No one outside the orphanage knew or learned of these travesties for over two hundred years. What caused this lunacy? Was it the devil or other dark forces?

Since the dawn of time, man has looked to the heavens, an unreachable space filled with mysterious order and wonder. All the visible heavenly bodies have been used to schedule planting and harvest, navigate the seas, and to prophesy future events. In particular, the moon, more than just a calendar in the sky, often has been a harbinger of the inevitable.

The moon, our closest celestial body, has always provided a fascination, and basis for the subject of legends and myths. Human behavior has been blamed on the lunar effects of some people's moods, thinking, or actions. People have been labeled "lunatics" because of this seeming loss of rational control of their actions at times near a full moon event.

Modern studies have tried to debunk the "lunatic" effect by studying thousands of cases of abnormal behavior reported at hospitals and clinics. Many studies saw significantly more patients with personality disorders during the twelve hours and twenty-four hours prior to and following the full moon. Certain activities considered "lunacy" in mental hospital admissions, psychiatric disturbances, crisis calls, homicides, and other criminal offenses could be attributed to the full moon, albeit in only about one percent of the case studies. Ah, but the one percent, the one percent happened in Philadelphia in 1883.

There's a Harvest Moon, a Blood Moon, a Super Moon, a Snow Moon, and every so often a Blue Moon, and many more named full moons. Perhaps lurking somewhere within the one percent of all full moons, there are spiritual forces of evil—evil forces of a Devil Moon.

Yes, a Devil Moon rose over Philadelphia in October 1883.

There was also a Devil Moon over a small orphanage near Glasgow in 1784. The Presbyterian Church took charge of any church members who were illegitimate fornicators. Normally, a family would raise the child; but if they were church members, the church elders decided the fate.

The woman of an illegitimate child was forced to confess her immorality in front of the church body to eradicate the taint of her moral contagion. More often than not, the mother was sent to an asylum, and put in solitary confinement for three months to think about her transgression and pray for forgiveness. Many of the mothers were prostitutes, but many were just guilty of unwed motherhood.

When the child was born, it was sent to an orphanage.

"For our struggle is not against
flesh and blood...but against the powers
of this dark world and the spiritual
forces of evil in the heavenly realms."

Ephesians 6:12, Holy Bible
New International Version

CHAPTER 1

Glasgow, Scotland
The Great Escape
Sunday, January 4, 1778
Possolpairk
12:00 Noon

The clock tower chimed noon as icy snow covered the city and the surrounding landscape. It was a particularly frigid winter for Glasgow.

David McNally was walking home from church with Catherine Farber and their families, as they did most Sundays. David was smitten by Catherine, just fourteen. The young couple met at a Presbyterian church on the north bank of the River Clyde, not far from the neighborhood in which they lived, a poor area of the city called Possolpairk. David, sixteen, worked with his father, Daniel, at a weaving mill, where Catherine also worked alongside her older sister, Ailena. David never knew his mother, who died of yellow fever with her unborn child when David was very young. Catherine's father died of smallpox when she was twelve. The girls' mother, Davina, worked at home as a dressmaker and seamstress. Both families attended the local church every Sunday. Daniel and Davina became close after the death of Davina's husband, although they had not married.

Catherine was a pretty, petite girl with long reddish hair, her complexion was very fair, and her face was dotted with freckles complementing her sparkling blue-green eyes. She had a soft, gentle voice, which made her all the more attractive. David was tall and

11

muscular with a ruddy complexion and a tight curly blond head of hair. He spoke with a deep voice, and he always had a charming smile with a bit of a twinkle in his bright blue eyes. His hands were large and scarred from the hard work at the mill where he cleaned the looms and other equipment.

On this particular Sunday, David asked Catherine if she would like to take a walk down to the river to see the new dock construction that had just started.

David's father, Daniel, a rugged man with dark circles under his eyes and a crooked mouth from an accident at the mill, looked much older than his thirty-six years. "You youngsters mind yerself out there now," he said with a grin.

The young couple walked along the banks of the Clyde to the Hutchenson Street Bridge, which overlooked the new Queen's Dock project. The construction had been going on for months, along with the deepening of the Clyde channel. David took pride in telling Catherine his knowledge of the work being done.

"Ya see those stone walls going into the river at an angle? Just there...from both sides," he said, pointing to the stoneworks. "When the current goes through that opening in the middle, it runs fast and washes the bottom, making the channel deeper. They will move the stones further down the river in about six months."

Catherine was impressed with his knowledge.

"How do you know such things?" Catherine asked.

"I come here after work some days and talk with the workers. You know how I like to talk with people, ya know, and I just have a curiosity about most things, I do."

Week after week, David and Catherine would walk in the crisp winter cold and talk as they walked after church. Catherine was more the listener, and David more of a talker. They were falling in love.

During the last week in March, David had something special in mind, and so on the last Sunday in March, on their usual walk, he stopped and put his hands on the shoulders of her coat. He told Catherine he loved her and wanted to marry her. Catherine blushed but smiled and stepped back slightly, not knowing what to say, although she knew how she felt. "How can we do that? Where will we live? I'm not sure our parents will approve. I have so many questions."

David paused for a moment and said, "Somehow, we will figure this out. We will. I have Friday afternoon free from my work. The mill is shutting down for some repairs. Could you walk with me again on Friday?"

"I will, David, I will."

All week long, David and Catherine tried to fight off the big questions of how a marriage could happen for them. How could they afford to do what they wanted without shirking their family responsibilities? There seemed to be no good answers.

Friday, March 6, 1778, by the River Clyde, late in the afternoon, David and Catherine met down by the river at the path where they always started their Sunday walks; the sky was cloudy, and the air frigid. Light windblown snow started to fall.

"It really doesn't look like a good day for a walk," David said, "but we need to talk. I know of a vacant tenement house just across the river. We can go there and get out of the weather. It's not a far walk. The tenants moved out last week, and the new folks won't move in for a month or so."

David had been to the house earlier that day, entering through a back door that was left unlocked. The tenants, in their move, left a good pile of firewood, so he made a fire to warm the hearth and take the chill from the room. He set down some blankets on the hearth and went off to meet Catherine.

When David and Catherine arrived at the tenement house, the sky was getting dark, and the snow was coming down heavier. It was cold icy snow. The snow pellets stung as they bounced off their cheeks.

They approached the tenement house and went in through the back door. The room was small and warm. The shutters on the two front windows were closed, but the room was glowing from the bright embers in the fireplace.

When Catherine saw all this, she just giggled and threw her arms around him and said, "I love you, David McNally." David put some more logs on the embers. The fire came alive. They made love for the first time. David was gentle and kind, and Ann responded with quiet moans of joy. "David, I do love you so much, but I don't know how we can go about getting married. It all seems so impossible."

"Catherine, my dearest, I know the good Lord will show us the way. He will now. He will."

They continued to use their love nest in the tenement house for the next several months, and then their regular plans of meeting there stopped when the new tenants moved in. But they continued their Sunday walks, talking about a future they dreamed about and not knowing how or when it could happen.

One Sunday at church, a friend of Catherine's, Alia, was summoned by the minister to confess to the congregation her sins of the flesh. She was an unwed mother. The young woman was chastised by the priest. She said she did not know who the father was, which only made her case worse. David and Catherine watched and listened in shock as this drama unfolded. It was to go on for three weeks—three weeks of public confession and scolding. During this time, Alia was forbidden to speak to anyone except to beg forgiveness and express her guilt.

On their walk after church that day, it was a beautiful spring day, filled with the smell of fresh grasses and early wildflowers along the river pathway and into the surrounding fields.

"David, I am very frightened."

"Why?"

"I've missed my time this month. I think I am with our child. I am so scared. I don't want to go through what happened to Alia at church today. I can't do that. I won't do that," she said.

"Catherine, what we saw today is a sign from the Lord, a sign that what we want to do is right for us. You will have our child, and we will get married. I will make a plan. Please trust me. I love you. Just do not tell another soul about the child. Nothing is showing on you right now, so pray for our plan."

During the week, Alia did see Catherine. They met in secrecy in the village hay barn. Alia just kept crying and sobbing and fell to her knees, looking up at Catherine, saying, "Catherine, will you forgive me?"

14

"Of course, I will, Alia. Is John the father?"

"Yes."

Catherine helped Alia up and hugged her warmly, and said, "Alia, I will tell you, you and John must run away, and do not tell anyone, not even me, where you are going. You must do that. The church is not right in what they are doing. May God forgive me, but I am sure our God wants you to have and raise that child. Please do what I say."

"I will talk to John about what you said."

If not for her family belonging to the church, Alia would have had other options, like having her family raise the bastard child, albeit her family would be looked down on by the church and church members. Being a church member, Alia did not have that option available. The church elders made the decisions, not the family.

Alia did not run away with John. She was more willing to accept the horrible known than a very uncertain unknown. She continued going to church and took the full treatment. The minister called on God to curse her and the devil child within her. David and Catherine sat in silence, trying not to believe these words of hatred and scorn. As the tribunal ended, Alia was sent to an asylum, where she would give birth. Twelve months later, the child would be sent to a small orphanage in Lanark, Lanarkshire, just south of Glasgow.

After church, they walked the pathway along the Clyde for the last time. "I am very frightened," said Catherine.

"Catherine, we both saw and heard what went on in the church. I cannot have you go through that, nor will I. We must leave this place." David laid out his plan. "Next Thursday, a sailing ship, the Amanda, is leaving City Dock at six thirty in the morning, on the outgoing tide, for Dublin, Ireland. I have already bought our ticket contract and listed us as husband and wife. I have saved up enough money to keep us until I can find work and a place for us to stay. We will need to leave early. It's a two-mile walk to the ship, and we can't miss it. I will meet you right after the four o'clock clock tower chime, down by the river, so stay awake and listen for the chime. Take warm clothes and whatever else you can carry. Wrap it all up in a wool blanket."

David spoke with such assurance that all would go well. "One other thing. Write a letter to your mum and sister telling them we are going away to get married and that we will one day return. I will do the same for my father and post it the day before we leave."

"I will," said Catherine. And so it was. The adventure of a lifetime was unfolding faster than they could believe.

Thursday, June 11, 1778

The clock tower chimed 4:00 a.m.

The sky was aglow with stars reaching down to the skyline of the city, and as the couple walked across the bridge of seven stone arches, they approached the City Dock. The sky suddenly brightened as a huge full moon rose on the horizon. The river had a few sailing ships at the dock; they wondered which one was the Amanda. The tide had started going out several hours ago; they could see the moving current in the moonlit ripples of the river.

The City Dock was illuminated by both the rising full moon and by rows of hanging oil lamps along the wharf. Walking past the first few boats, they saw the Amanda, on their way to a new life; it gave them a rush of hope. The name of the ship was barely readable, as the painted letters on the bow had faded over the years. The Amanda was a twenty-five-year-old three-masted sailing ship that had been regularly making round trips to Dublin and Belfast, carrying both passengers and cargo. The lines of the sailing ship were sleek, but its design did not compliment the condition. She looked uncared for, lacking in paint and repairs, with tattered lines. The wheelhouse was missing a window, and the door was hanging from one hinge. It was obvious that no money was put into maintaining the vessel.

The ship timed its departures and arrivals with both the rapid outgoing and incoming tides of the River Clyde in Glasgow and the River Liffey in Dublin. The trip across the Irish Sea would last all night, all through the early morning darkness, arriving at Dublin harbor about twenty-two hours later the next morning.

Workmen were busy loading barrels and boxes by way of the stern gangplanks, and passengers were boarding closer to the bow.

David had his ticket contract in hand as the couple came aboard the ship. The captain signed the ticket paper and told David he would need this to disembark in Dublin.

"Unless you have an 'enclosed passage' ticket, yer to remain on the deck. Ya can find a place up near the foremast. There's fresh water in the barrels and chamber pots with lines attached to the rail. Now ya give 'em a good ocean wash when yer done," the captain said to the large group huddled near the gangway.

Many of the passengers were confined to the open deck, as the deck below was for the more expensive "enclosed passage" ticket holders only, and below that was a cargo deck. There were about one hundred people, young and old, crowded on the deck when the gangplanks were removed; the docking lines were heaved aboard and stowed. As soon as the lines were stowed, the Amanda drifted slowly out into the mainstream current of the Clyde. A crew of six made ready the sails as the Amanda drifted toward the sea. The sails were tattered and filled with unrepaired tears and covered with a multitude of makeshift patches.

David and Catherine, and most of the other on-deck passengers looked back as the Glasgow skyline receded in the distance.

In about an hour, the mouth of the river suddenly widened as the Amanda made a gradual turn to the south into the Firth of Clyde. In another hour, still heading south, they entered the North Channel leading to the Irish Sea. The day was bright but now very overcast, with low clouds and a steady wind out of the northwest. The sails were full, and the following sea brought wave after wave into the starboard quarter of the ship, causing both pitching and rolling, the perfect recipe for seasickness.

The captain warned all passengers to "make a hold to the ship, for if ye go overboard, ye will be lost for sure." David and Catherine were on a small-raised platform around the foremast, where the motions of the ship were some of the worst. David piled some of the docking lines over their wool blankets to keep them by the mast and from sliding onto the wet deck. They were so sick; having had nothing to eat that morning, they could not even vomit, only constantly wretch.

After about three dreadful hours of this, the seas finally settled, and David and Catherine were able to eat some of the small loaves of bread David had brought for the voyage. Their "mal de mer" finally left. They had their "sea legs."

David looked at the sky and thought to himself, *Thank you, dear Lord, for your deliverance. Please stay with us, care for us, and bless our child.* Exhausted from the emotions and events of the day, they both remained silent as they huddled together, wrapped in their blankets, which they pulled over their heads to block the constant spray from the bow wake. They finally found sleep as the sun sank below the horizon in a brilliant red sky.

CHAPTER 2

Ireland
A Pilgrimage with No Return
Friday, June 12, 1778

D avid woke up just as dawn was breaking. In spite of the ocean spray and cool air, he felt warm next to Catherine under the wool blankets. He looked around and saw there were already a few people stirring about on the deck, most standing by the rail, looking ahead for the sight of land.

He slowly slipped out of their blankets and stood up, looking down at Catherine with a smile as she slept by his feet. All of a sudden, there was a cheer from those on watch at the bow.

"There 'tis. There 'tis!"

Catherine was wakened by the cheers. She sat up and gave David's legs a big hug.

"Did you sleep well, darl'n'?"

"I woke up a few times with the worries on me mind, but I did sleep."

"We're almost there, Catherine," he said, looking down at her with a smile. He reached down and helped her to her feet.

As the sun peeked over the port horizon into a brilliantly clear morning sky, all the passengers were now standing along the starboard rail, looking to the southwest as the port of Dublin came into view.

It took several hours to maneuver the ship with the now light northwesterly winds and the incoming tide. At last, the Amanda passed the Poolbeg Lighthouse at the end of the Great South Wall at the harbor entrance.

David was fascinated with the lighthouse design. It was rather squat-looking, about ten meters wide at the base, eight meters wide at the top, and twenty meters high, topped with a dome light. Vertical lines of windows ran up the sides to illuminate the stairway inside.

Both the lighthouse and the almost four-kilometer-long Great South Wall were completed several years before as a breakwater to protect incoming ships from wind and waves when entering the mouth of the River Liffey into Dublin Harbor.

The Amanda drifted toward the South Wall docking area, where there were mooring buoys about fifty meters outward from the wall in the channel.

The mainsails were lowered, and the buoys snagged as the deck crew attached lines both fore and aft. Once tied off, the ship stopped drifting. The crew cast a cargo net over the port side gangway for disembarkation. Longboats approached the Amanda and, one by one, tied off to the cargo net as the passengers climbed down. Older passengers were lowered in a makeshift boatswain's chair from a davit that swung out over the side above the awaiting boats.

"All deck passengers disembark," cried the captain. "Welcome to Dublin. We need deck space, so move lively now."

The deck passengers and mail went on the longboats, which were rowed to the Dublin City docks. The below-deck passengers would remain on the ship in relative comfort until the ship reached the dock in the city. The ship would take a few more hours to complete the trip in the slow-moving tide; the captain did not opt to pay for a steam-driven tug to haul him into the port.

While en-route, the crew transferred the cargo to the top deck.

David and Catherine were in the first longboat. The sight of the Dublin waterfront was not very inviting. The wharves and docks were crowded with sailing ships lined up cheek to jowl, loaded with crates, sacks, barrels, and other cargo.

When they first stepped onto Irish soil, they walked through a wet, stinking mixture of garbage and manure that covered most of the cobblestone pavement.

Many goods were coming in and going out. Hundreds of workmen milled back and forth, on and off the ships, all with the constant din of men shouting and the sound of horses' hoofs and iron-rimmed carriage wheels on the stone block wharves.

There was an array of impressive limestone buildings at the end of the harbor. One was clearly marked "Customs House." It was several stories tall with a large dome on top.

Catherine reached into her bundle of clothing and found the letter to her mother. Amazingly, it was still dry after the wet night at sea. "We must follow the man with the mailbag," said Catherine. "This is the letter to my mum you asked me to write. I did'na have time t'post it yesterday."

As they followed the postman toward the custom's house, they overheard many people speaking, some in English, some in Irish, and some in Gaelic. One good thing they got from their church school in Glasgow was the ability to read, write, and speak both Gaelic and English.

They followed the postman into the building. It was cold inside and dimly lit only by sunlight through the windows. The interior limestone mimicked the exterior design, with five-meter-high ceilings; they walked down a wide hallway where the sound of theirs, and the feet of many others, on the stone floors echoed loudly. They finally reached a door marked with a sign overhead "Royal Mail."

Catherine stopped by the doorway and unfolded the letter to her mother.

"Here, David, I want ya t'read my letter."

He took the letter. It was written in ink, and it had some spots where the ink ran when Catherine's tears fell on it as she wrote. David read it:

Dearest Mother,

I am sorry if I made you worry about my quick disappearance, but it is something I had to do. Daniel is with me.

We are safe and happy. We are getting married and having a child. I could not face the scorn of the church nor the thought of losing our child or spending my life in an asylum. Please forgive me for leaving you and Ailena. We must start this new life together.

I will try my best to make it a happy one, and I hope someday I will see you again.

Your loving daughter,
Catherine Ann

She took the letter, sealed it in an envelope, and handed it to the postmaster.

"One letter t' Glasgow. That'll be eight pennies fer postage, Miss."

David reached into his pocket for a few coins.

"Did ya young folks jus' arrive on the Amanda from Scotland?" the postmaster asked.

"Aye, we did," said David.

"Do ya have yer' signed ship tickets?" the postmaster asked.

"Aye, we do."

"Ya will need to give 'em t'da clerk at d'desk near d'fr'nt door."

"We will," said David, but he did not turn in the arrival papers. He was afraid that somehow their path might be traced.

When they left the customs house, it didn't take David long to figure out they had to get out of this part of the city. He watched as hordes of men loaded up wagons with boxes and barrels.

He listened in on their conversations, which were mostly in English and Irish. He would occasionally inquire to an English-speaking driver as to where they were going and what kind of place that might be. Many of the coach drivers had no time for him.

"Mind yerself, lad. I'm busy," one of them uttered. Others spent time talking about the places they were going to in Dublin City, the surrounding countryside, and beyond.

David finally asked one of the coach drivers, who seemed a friendly chap, "Me wife and me need t'go to d'place where you are going, the place just outside d'city you jus' told me about. We want to find work and find a place where we can start a family. Would ya, for a few shillings, allow us ta ride on your wagon with you, now would ya?"

"Better den dat, lad, if y'd help me load me wagon, th'll be no charge."

"I will. Thank ya," said David. "By d'by, what's yer name?" David asked.

"Well, me full name is Patrick James McFarlin. Ya can jus' call me Patrick James McFarlin," he said with a hearty laugh. "Jes' call me Pat."

David laughed with him and said, "Fine, Pat, let me get started load'n d'wagon."

Pat sat on the seat of the wagon and motioned to David just how he wanted the wagon loaded. There were wooden boxes and barrels and sacks of grain and even two wagon wheels and several bolts of fabric. Pat told David to take the two long boards from under the wagon and use them to roll the heavy cargo and barrels up into the wagon. Once loaded, David helped Catherine up on top of the load onto a soft grain bag.

And so it was. They started their journey from Dublin Harbor to the open farmlands on the outskirts of the city in search of a home.

Pat followed the dirt road along the south side of the River Liffey, heading to the northwest. The road was in terrible disrepair, with mud holes and ruts, making for a very slow trip, lest the wheels or, worse, an axil might break. Pat made a few stops in the city on some side streets, and David offloaded boxes and sacks of grain. They got back on the main road and left the city.

About two kilometers out of the city, the worst did happen— the front left wagon wheel went into a deep pothole. The wagon lurched to the left, throwing Pat from the wagon onto the side of the road.

"Fer Chris' sake!" he yelled as he hit the ground.

Catherine was knocked from her perch on the grain sack onto the floor of the wagon. David managed to hold on. There was a loud distinctive "crack" as the wagon listed sharply to the left. The front axil had snapped just inside the wheel. This all happened in a few seconds. It was so loud that it sent the horse into a gallop, which was slowed by the wagon scraping its front end into the road.

David looked at Catherine. She seemed unhurt.

He hollered, "Hang on!" He dove forward and grabbed the reins. "Whoa, fella, whoa!" The horse stopped. It was all over.

"Catherine, are ya hurt?"

"No, just a bit shaken up."

"Pat, are ya all right?"

"Jus' a few bruises."

David and Pat assessed the damages.

"What a bloody mess dis be," said Pat.

"How far to the village from here?" asked David.

"Bout five K."

"We can fix this so we can get there," said David. "If we off-load the cargo, we can remove both front wheels and rig up a skid under the front of the carriage using the loading planks."

In about two hours, they were on the move, a lot slower, a sorry sight, but on their way, nonetheless, scraping their way down the road in the now part sled, part wagon.

An hour later, Pat stopped so the horses could have a drink of water, where the road forded a small stream.

"Tis w'd be a goot place for ya two to clean up a bit. Ya' both look a mess, now, ya do," Pat said with a laugh.

"You're a sorry sight yerself," said David.

David helped Catherine off the wagon and brought out the remaining hard bread he had in his sack. He dipped it in the stream, and they ate and drank the cold clear water. They used a few clean rags they packed to wash up. It felt so good after the long night at sea and the events of the day.

The scene was ever-changing as the wagon slowly made its way further north into the countryside. The repair was holding and doing its job.

"So, Catherine, are ya' feel'n a bit better now, seeing 'n this nice countryside? Are ya' now?" asked David.

"Yes, but I'm still full of d'worries. I'm hopin' and pray'n that somethin' good will happen when we reach d'village. It sounded so nice, and I jus' hope it is."

"I understand yer worries. I've a few too, but we must keep d'faith."

They traveled on, making a sharp left turn onto a much narrower road. The painted road sign pointed toward the village, "Baile Thormaid, 1 Km."

"You can git off anywhere here or ride with me to d'village center where ye might find a place to stay and maybe find some work."

"We'll stay on," said David. "I want to do the rest of d'unload'n for ya and, as I said, help ya with d'wagon repairs."

"No worries 'bout d'repairs. You will have enough to do."

Baile Thormaid was unlike anything they had seen in Scotland.

Today, the town is called Ballyfermot. The name is derived from the Middle Irish *baile*, meaning "farmstead."

It was a small village surrounded by small farms. Its town center was dominated by a modestly sized stone church crowned with a simple gable roof.

The dirt streets were wider than the city streets they knew in Glasgow and were lined with shops and cottages. Rows of mature sycamore trees surrounded the village square and lined the side streets.

The cottages were made mostly of stone. Some made all the sod and all with just one window. Very few of them had glass, as it was a luxury. They had sloping gable roofs of thatch or sod. Some had stone chimneys, but most just had smoke holes in the thatch for venting the cooking hearth below.

Outside the village were small farms with modest farmhouses and a few outbuildings. Mainly cows and horses grazed in the many pastures. Some had sheep and goats.

At the village square, David thanked the driver and said, "We'll first go and find d'church an d'minister."

The driver chuckled and said, "I wish ye both a good life. The church is just there. When ya meet the parish pastor, call him Pastor. Dat's what he goes by. Perhaps I'll see ya' both on another trip here to da' village. Fer now, goodbye."

They all waved goodbye.

The stone church was set up on the rise, overlooking the town square; it was a short walk and nearly six o'clock in the evening.

As they got closer, many other townspeople were also heading for the church. The pastor stood by the front door, ringing the cloche or handbell, summoning the brethren to worship. David and Catherine's hearts were full of hope and joy at the sight and sound.

They had never seen a church like this. The sign in front read:

> The Church of Ireland at Baile Thormaid
> Sean Gregor, Pastor
> Sunday Service, 8 o'clock morning
> Weekdays, 6 o'clock evening

As they entered, the pastor greeted them with a simple "welcome," a smile, and a nod.

They filed in with the locals who all gave them curious glances; most smiled, and some just a nod of recognition as strangers.

They sat in the back on a bench with their bundles on the floor. David and Catherine liked this church and felt a certain warmth from the onlooker's reactions to them and the deep friendly tone of the pastor's voice.

Nothing like this existed in Glasgow. It was a blend of Methodist and Catholic religions.

The regular six o'clock service was a welcoming feeling for David and Catherine, so different, yet parts familiar, from the church in Glasgow.

After the service, they went out the front doors and saw the pastor walking up a path along the side of the church toward the clergy house. They quickly followed him.

"Oh, Pastor!" called David.

The pastor stopped and turned and saw these apparent waifs at the door.

As they approached him, they stopped and just stared at him, holding their bundles of clothes, not really knowing what to say. Pastor Gregor was sixty-eight years old, short and rotund, with thin gray hair and bright blue eyes; his lips were narrow, closed, and expressionless.

"Yes, me son and daughter, what c'n I do for yas?"

"Pastor, we jus' came here across d'sea from Glasgow. We want to make a home here 'n raise a family. We want t'be part of your church. Pastor, may we join your church?"

"Well, now slow down, me boy, slow down. It will take a bit a' lessons, but, yes, dat can happen."

"Oh, thank you, Pastor," they said together.

"Where will you be stay'n in d'village? D'ya have relatives here?"

"We di'na have a place, Pastor. We di'na know one soul here. We need a place ta stay, and I need some work, and we need t'get married, all those things," said David.

"Well, young man and young lady, we've a lot a work t'do now, don't we? Ya both come with me now. We need t'talk a bit."

They followed the pastor to the Clergy House, a small cottage behind the church. They spent a lot of time speaking to Pastor Gregor and telling him of their lives in Glasgow, about their jobs, their church, and their families. They told him what happened to Catherine's friend at church, and with tears and sobs, Catherine told the pastor she was with their child and why they chose to flee Glasgow, leaving their parents behind.

The pastor listened intently. "Now, now, me child, no need t'cry now. I am here t'help ya, not t'punish ya, or you, David, or your child."

Catherine looked up with tears streaming down her cheeks and said, "Many thanks to you, Pastor Gregor. Thank you so much."

"David and Catherine, I'm an old man. I've been with this church since a child. I've seen so many changes. To me, d'changes have been for d'good over d'years for both d'people and d'church. Now d'Church of Ireland is more forgiv'n and more for help'n everyone when possible. I was just thinking this morning in my prayer time, 'Now what do ya have for me t'do for you today, Lord?' I will tell ya, I tink da good Lord has sent you t'me today with a lot t'do, and I will do those t'ings. I'll be retir'n as pastor later next year, so I want t'do what I can now for d'church and for yas, young people.

I will marry yas. I will marry yas right now with d'bless'n of Almighty God. Mr. O'Sullivan, our clergyman, keeps our church record and is working at the church now. We will go there. He and his wife will be your witnesses."

They went to the church and found Cormac O'Sullivan in a small room at the back of the church. He was shuffling some papers on his desk.

"Mr. O'Sullivan, I would like ya t'meet these fine young folks who wish t'get married 'n join our church. I would like you and Roisin t'be d'witnesses. Would ya kindly go across the street and bring her here?"

"Yes, just now, Sean, I will." Cormac Sullivan, while he thought this seemingly rushed wedding was unusual, he never questioned the pastor on anything, and he was not going to start now.

Cormac and Roisin O'Sullivan were in their late sixties, and not only had they been in this church all their lives, they knew Sean Gregor all their lives. He was their dearest and best friend.

When the O'Sullivans returned, the pastor took a prayer book from his pocket and, right then and there, married them.

"Kindly take care of the usual records, Cormac."

"Certainly, Sean."

"It will give much pleasure to introduce Mr. and Mrs. David McNally to our congregation at tomorrow's service. I'm sure ya two will be there."

"Oh, yes, we will," said David.

"But for now, we need t'get you some food and drink. We'll go back to the clergy house." They all walked through a misty, light rain, and they followed the pastor into the house.

"Come with me to my pantry."

The pastor set out some biscuits and cheese and poured water from a pitcher. He said a blessing, and they all ate at his table.

"For tonight, you c'n stay in my front room, 'n tomorrow, we'll find some work 'n a place for you both t'stay. But perhaps before ya git some sleep, you might want t'wash up a bit. Forgive me, but ya both are in need a good wash'n," he said with a jolly laugh.

David and Catherine laughed with him.

"You have both had a couple of busy days. There's a chang'n shed behind d'clergy house with a pump, basin, and some clean washing cloths. You'll find it just there"—he pointed—"just out back. I will see you both in d'morn'n, and we'll see 'bout find'n a place t'stay 'n some good work for you, David. God bless ya both 'n good night."

The pastor retired to his room.

After they washed up and changed, they spread the blankets on the floor of the clergy house front room and quickly fell into a much-needed sleep; they were both physically and mentally exhausted.

CHAPTER 3

Baile Thormaid
1778

D avid woke up just before dawn. He had a real urge to pee,
so he quickly and quietly went to the back door to relieve
himself.

The sun was still below the horizon, but the sky was brightening
by the minute. In some ways, the last sunrise he saw while on the
Amanda yesterday seemed long ago, as so much had happened
yesterday. He looked around; he could see three houses across the
field behind the clergy house that looked like they might be small
farms. The scene was quite pastoral, with a light haze on the meadows
and the sound of early birds.

Catherine opened the back door, looking for David.

"It's right here," David said with a laugh. "Isn't this just a
beautiful place, Catherine?"

"For sure…'tis very beautiful."

A few moments later, the pastor was up and leaning out the
back door. "I thought you would be need'n and finding d'little house.
Now come in now. I have some cheese 'n bread 'n hot tea for you."

After a blessing, they ate their breakfast, which tasted like the
best food they had ever eaten.

The pastor spoke, "Well now, I have a young couple who
belong to our church I'd like you t'meet. They have a small farm,
raise potatoes 'n a few other vegetables 'n have a few cows, some
sheep, and a horse. I've been tink'n they need some extra help. When

last I spoke wid Connor and Aisling McGowan, I inquired how d'farm work was go'n. I sensed they felt overworked 'n couldn't find any local help. Everyone 'n d'village and in d'surround'n farms have work. Most have large families t'do da work. The McGowans only have one young daughter, barely a year old now, who takes up a lot of Aisling's time, so she has little time t'help Connor with d'farm. We shall go 'n talk with 'em now, we will, we will. Let's go."

Pastor Gregor led them out the front door of the clergy house and down the road to the east of the town center.

"That's their cottage and barn over there."

As they got closer, they could see Connor McGowan working in a fenced pasture by the barn, feeding the cows and sheep. Aisling was in front of the cottage and appeared to be nursing her baby.

"Top of the mornin', Connor!" the pastor shouted with a wave.

"D'same t'ya!" hollered Collin, waving back.

"An a good morn'n, Aisling!" the pastor shouted with another wave, seeing Aisling and her baby sitting in front of their cottage.

They walked up to the pasture fence. "Who are your friends, Pastor?"

"I'd like ya t'meet David and Catherine McNally. You probably noticed 'em in church yesterday. They jus' got here from Scotland, and they want to settle in our town, join our church, and start a family."

"Well, good t'meet ya," Connor said with a nod. "I did see ya yesterdee. So, Pastor, why d'special visit?" asked Connor.

"The last I spoke wid you and Aisling, ye told me the work at d'farm was gett'n a bit much for ya now that Aisling has t'spend so much time with the baby. By the way, how is Ciara?"

"She's just fine and the joy of our hearts. We are blessed, Pastor. We are truly blessed," Connor said with a smile of pride.

"So when this young couple spoke to me after the service yesterday, I thought of you and Aisling. I thought these folks might be able t'lend a hand. They both have farm experience from back in Scotland."

"Aye, we do," said Daniel humbly. "We would do whatever you need us to do to help you and your wife. We just need some shelter and food."

"I'm afraid we d'na have any wages t'pay ya."

"No need for wages," David said. "We just need a place to stay and work for our keep."

Connor thought in silence for a while, pursing his lips, and put his right hand on his chin.

David and Catherine waited hopefully for a reply.

After a short pause, the pastor said, "Well now, Connor, that jus' might be d't'ing ya might need right now. What d'ya t'ink?"

"Why don't we all go to d'cottage 'n we can talk wid Aisling about how this might work. She would have t'be in tot'l agreement," said Connor.

They walked to the cottage where Aisling was sitting on a stool by the front door. She was wearing a long white linen dress with buttons on the shoulder straps; she had finished nursing the baby.

Aisling spoke as they came closer, "Top of the morn' to you all. I saw you and these folks come'n up d'road and go'n over t'talk with Connor. Is everything all right?"

"Everything is fine," said Connor. "Pastor Gregor brought the folks here, who are new to the village, here t'meet us."

"Yes, I saw you both at church yesterday," said Aisling.

"I s'pose everyone did," said Catherine shyly.

"The pastor brought 'em here t'meet us. He knows we need help, and they need work. They both know farm'n, and Catherine is a good dressmaker as well. They need a place t'stay and won't charge for wages."

"How d'ya know farm work?" Aisling asked.

"We both did farm work for our families in Scotland, and Catherine is a good dressmaker, and I know how t'repair 'most anything."

"I'll be go'n back to d'church now. I have work t'do. I'll leave you all here, 'n I hope some good t'ings will work out," said the pastor.

The two couples talked for quite some time. They seemed to have the same values and goals in life. Connor finally spoke.

"David could fix up space in the old horse barn for them. You know, we do need help, and, in this short time together, we seem t'get along just fine."

Connor looked at Catherine. She nodded. "So you will join our farm right now if you want to, all right?"

"Many t'anks. We'll both work hard and earn our keep," said David.

"Do you have some things ya need t' bring here?" asked Connor.

"Just a few things we left back at the clergy house. I can get 'em later 'n tell the pastor the good news," said David.

"Well, for now, come with me. You can help me finish up milk'n d'cows, and then we c'n go take a look at d'barn. Catherine, why don't you go inside with Aisling 'n Ciara."

From March 1778 through June, the weather remained cool and comfortable in Baile Thormaid. David pitched right in, working long hours on the McGowan farm. Catherine was a constant companion of Aisling, helping her with chores and sewing new clothing for Ciara, who was growing by the day. Connor told David for the first month, he should work to get their quarters in the barn in order, and he did.

There was a supply of enough sawn planks, nails, and a few rusty tools that David cleaned and sharpened, but the job got done and quickly. Connor was impressed with the quality of the work and the speed at which it was done, given the lack of better tools.

David partitioned off a small space in the back of the barn for their room and built a back door, and added one window without glass, as that was too expensive to buy, then added shutters with hinges. He fashioned them out of some old harness leather he found in the barn. Shutters were a must and needed for the window to keep out the winter cold and bad weather.

On the back wall, he constructed a sizable fireplace with a hearth for the room from flat rocks that he gathered from the surrounding pastures. The rocks were cleverly fitted together with just thin layers of sod and no benefit of actual mortar. A chimney went up between the barn support poles of the back wall.

The room and fireplace were finished in less than two weeks' time. Connor, on seeing this, asked David to add a chimney to the cooking hearth in their cottage to replace the smoke hole, which he did.

During this time, David built a chimney for not only Connor's cottage but also a rocking crib for Ciara, while Catherine sewed a cover for a lambswool pad.

Both the cottage and the barn room were simple spaces with hardened clay floors, a small table, and two wooden chairs. Beds were wooden, raised platforms only a half meter from the floor. Straw was used for bedding, mixed with the scraps of unsaleable lamb shearlings, all covered with old blanket cloth, to finish the sleeping surface.

David and Catherine really liked being on the farm, and the routine of the daily work was predictable. It was the same every day, except Sundays, when they went to church. Father, Sean, as they called him, became a best friend.

Often the good father would come to the farm and talk with the women for an hour and then find the men and talk with them as they worked. They always gave the good father a basket of vegetables and some fresh milk or butter.

By July, the weather got muggy as the days drifted into a hot summer. The farm was doing very well, mostly because of David's efforts. The profits from the sale of milk and produce were more than twice from last year, a windfall that Connor could not ignore, and knowing why it was so. It was all because of David's work.

David was first up each morning, milking the cows and turning them out. David was eager and learned all about potato farming, the main crop on Connor's farm. David also shared his family farming experience in Scotland, where they did not raise potatoes but turnips and beets.

By the fall of 1778, small fields of these were added to the McGowan farm. Once harvested, they were placed in a shallow root cellar next to the Connors' cottage.

By the end of the summer, Catherine was very large with the baby, and, at the same time, Aisling was pregnant with her second child. Catherine and Aisling spent a lot of time together and became very good friends.

September 15th was a cool night. Catherine gave birth to her child in their room in the barn. It was late in the evening. Aisling was there to help with the birthing, along with David and Connor. They were all around Catherine in the light of two oil lamps as she was going through labor. Just before the baby was delivered, a brighter light from the sky pierced the window of the barn, overpowering the light from the lamps. It fell on Catherine's belly. It was the light of a bright, reddish full moon that had just ascended.

David made a fire and heated some water to wash what needed washing. Catherine screamed with pain as the contractions continued. The baby came quickly. It was a boy.

The previous week, she and David heard the pastor give his sermon from the book of Luke. He told how Luke was a great physician and a man who loved the Lord. When Catherine saw the baby was a boy, she said, "David, I would like t'name our child Luke."

"Yes, it shall be," said David.

David tied off the cord and cut it and then washed the child and Catherine and dressed her in clean, warm clothes.

He wrapped his new son in soft clothes and placed him on Catherine's breast; she held him to her as he suckled her breast.

Connor and Aisling, seeing no more to be done, returned to their cottage.

By October, Connor decided to talk to David about the new success of the farm. "David, yer work here has b'n a bless'n. You've helped us get such a goot profit from d'farm. Because of dis, I want'a give ya a wage. Ya deserve it."

"Why, thank ya, Connor. That means a lot t'me. Whatever ya t'ink is right is goot fer me."

"I can afford to pay ya a penny a day."

As time went on, David kept all the wages, not knowing how he might need this newfound money; that time was coming sooner than he thought.

The winter crops were planted, and by December, winter set in. It was cold and damp, and there was not much outside work to be done at the farm other than fence repairs, for which David did most of the work. For the most part, the animals were kept in the barn and were fed with the hay stored in the loft above, another area of the barn David had repaired. The winter was long and cold.

Over the winter, some changes happened that were not to David's liking. One February Sunday, Pastor Gregor announced his retirement, explaining that he would be moving back to Dublin to be near the rest of his family. Both David and Catherine grieved that loss in their lives, even though they knew it was coming. That was the last day they went to church there.

David also started to resent that Connor had gotten into a habit of sleeping in a bit now that David was on the job. David was getting tired and annoyed that Connor seemed content to let him do more and more of the work.

By the beginning of March, the weather moderated, and the ground was made ready for planting the summer crops. At dawn, David was first, as usual, on the job, turning the cows out and loading the cart with potatoes for sale in the village. David had repaired this good-sized cart he found in the barn and was currently working on a larger broken-down wagon. The wagon was in decent shape, but two of the wheels had broken wooden spokes. He found a small oak tree, cut it, and with a rusty spokeshave that he cleaned and sharpened, he fashioned two new spokes. He had finished most of the work a few days ago.

Till now, the farm horse, a dappled gray swayback mare, was only used to pull the smaller cart to the market in the village. Soon the larger carriage would be ready for use. David also found the old leather harnesses in the barn, all in fairly good condition with just the need of some minor repairs: the apron, driving apron, turn back, bellyband, and the rest of the rigging. He had already repaired the horse harnesses and refurbished them with oil.

By this time, it was a cool March morning when Connor came into the barn where David had been working for the past three hours, working with a spokeshave, making the last replacement spoke for the wagon.

"Goot morn'n, David," said Connor.

"Oh, is it now?" said David, not looking up from his work.

"Do ye have a problem now, David, do ya? What kind of reply is dat to a goot morning?" said Connor.

David did not answer right away and just kept working. The work he was doing on the wagon was something that Connor could never have done. He knew that, and so did Connor.

"David, did ya hear me?" said Connor in a louder voice.

David looked up from his work and stared at Connor. David finally spoke, "Connor, yer lazy, you are, and I'm tired of doing all the work around here. We'll be leav'n here as soon as we can. We will leave this place. D'sooner, d'betta. I'll have no more of it."

Connor shouted back, "So that's how it is, is it? By d'morn'n, I want yas gone. D'ya hear me me now? I want yas gone from my farm."

David spoke with Catherine later in the day and that night. She was again filled with worries by David's news of what might be next, and now with her new son to take care of as well. She was happy with her life on Connor's farm, but David was not. They would be moving on.

David tried to assure her that all would be well, but she had doubts. He did, too, not knowing what was ahead, but he knew what they had to do. They had to leave this place behind and search for brighter pastures and hope for a geographical cure.

CHAPTER 4

1779
Broken Bliss to New Hope

W hen Connor told David he was to leave his farm in the morning, David, as usual, was quick to develop his own plan. He did not sleep that night. He told Catherine to pack their things in blankets and a canvas and to get what sleep she could.

"Well, how can we carry all our t'ings and Luke?"

"Leave that t'me. Just get some sleep. We'll be leav'n before dawn. I'll wake you when I'm ready to leave."

He had finished the minor repairs on the wagon, working through the night, getting the remaining wheel repaired and back in place. The wagon had a driver's seat and an open cart that sat on a carriage mounted above the rear wheels.

About an hour before dawn, David got the horse from the stable and rigged him with harnesses. He gave the horse a pile of hay to eat and a bucket of water and then went to the root cellar and got a supply of potatoes. He went to their room at the back of the barn, where Catherine was sound asleep with his son, Luke, who was now one year old. He collected a cooking pot and gathered most of their possessions, returned to the barn, and loaded the wagon, and then he went back to their room and awakened Catherine. "'Tis time, we must go now. Get a warm blanket for Luke and come into the barn."

The barn was dark except for the one oil lamp David had lit to hitch up the horse to the wagon.

When Catherine, with Luke in her arms, came into the barn, she was shocked at the sight. "David, what are you doing?"

"I'm doing what we have to do to get out of here."

"But we just can't take the horse and wagon. That's stealing."

"That bastard owes it to us." Catherine never saw this angry side of David or ever heard him use these kinds of words.

"Come now, you and Luke get up in d'wagon."

"I will not do it, David. I won't. I don't know where we are go'n, but we shall walk there. We shall walk if need be. We will not make this move from here as thieves. We will not!"

Just as Catherine was shocked at David's planned actions, David was shocked that she stood up to him.

David was frustrated and still angry. His lips were pursed with yet unvented anger. He looked at Catherine's eyes, which reflected the light of the oil lamp. She was staring at him in utter disbelief.

David broke his silence. "You are right. I am sorry. I'm jus' so angry with Connor. A big bosthoon he is. I can't work for him anymore. I can't. We shall walk out of here and head north up to County Armagh. I've heard they have a lot of good farm'n there. We will get there and find a place and good work."

David put the mare back in the stall and unloaded their belongings and the food he gathered for the journey.

When finished, he just stared at the large pile with his hands on his hips. For the first time, his mind drew a blank.

As the morning sun came up, long streaks of light came through the cracks in the barn doors, lighting up the dust in the dark air.

All at once, the doors opened. It was Connor. He took two steps into the barn and stopped, surprised to see David and Catherine standing over the pile of their possessions.

"David, I couldn't sleep. You's don't hav'ta leave." Connor had thought all night; he needed David to work the farm.

David did not answer and turned his eyes back to their pile of belongings. He finally turned to Connor.

"We be gone now," he said in a strong, assertive tone of voice.

David was stubborn and was not going to accept Connor's change of heart, as he knew if life continued here, it would be the same, him doing most of the work and with resentment.

"Me decision is made."

"All right then," said Connor. "But how will ye carry all yer t'ings?"

"I suppose we'll have to leave most of 'em."

Connor thought a moment and said, "Look now, I'll give yas d'small cart we been use'n to take our 'tatoes t'market."

David was too proud to give a thank you. He just continued staring at Connor while grinding his clenched teeth. Connor stared back for a while, then dropped his gaze. He turned and walked back to his cottage in silence. He looked back over his shoulder and said, "Take the cart. You earned it."

Catherine knew David would not change his mind, but she was relieved by Connor's offer of the cart.

"Go back to our room and gather what else we might need. I'll get the cart and load up our belongings and fix a spot for Luke."

They walked down the farm road toward the village, with David pulling the wagon. It was rigged with a leather harness that attached to a wide belt around David's waist.

They walked back to the main road, made a left turn, and started heading north. The road was narrow, rutted, and in total disrepair. It had a partly grassed center strip between the ruts made by larger wagons, which made for relatively comfortable walking, and a space wide enough for the smaller cart.

David led the way; Catherine followed in silence. After about two hours, David finally spoke,

"Catherine, I'm really sorry, me love. I am. Please forgive me. I didn't get any sleep last night. I am exhausted, and I need to catch a few winks."

They rested by the roadside for about an hour.

"Catherine, it's time t'move along."

They again walked in silence for about six more hours, passing only two small farm cottages with thatched roofs and small fields of potatoes. It was the custom for farmers to allow travelers to take a few from their fields that bordered a road, and David did just that.

Most of the road was bounded by heavy forest, and along the road, there were occasional fords across shallow streams and bogs, where stones had been placed to support wagon wheels.

"We'll stop here by this stream for a rest and have some bread and cheese," said David.

David spread a blanket and laid down with Catherine and Luke, and joined them in sleep. They were probably sleeping for about half an hour when they were awakened by a light but cold rain.

"Catherine, get up. I'll get some small canvases from the cart for Luke and us. We need to keep walking and try to stay dry."

They walked all day with just a few rest stops for water. At sunset, they stopped by a stream for water and washing and for an overnight stay.

David had packed a box of matches, wrapped in cloth, and stored them in a small metal tin. The rain had stopped hours ago, and it appeared that it didn't rain at all in this place. David was resourceful; he made a fire and had packed a small cooking tin, and had several potatoes and turnips in his pack. He boiled some turnip tops and found some muddy clay in the stream bank to cover a large potato, which he placed on the hot embers. The smell of the baked potato steaming made their mouths water.

After their daily meal, David built up the fire with the ample seasoned-dead branches at the edges of the road and covered his family with canvas squares. Sleep came fast.

This daily routine of walking, resting, and sleeping continued for seven days. At that time, they did not see another traveler or another wagon on the road, and they had no idea how far they had traveled. In fact, they covered about fifteen kilometers a day for a total of one hundred thirty kilometers by the time they reached the first sizable town on the eighth day.

At about noon that day, they approached another cottage near the road. A man was working in the garden. David left the road and approached him.

"Top'a tha'mor'n t'ya!" David shouted. The man responded in kind.

David asked the man how far it was to a village.

"About seven K to Doire Núis," he said.

Doire Núis was the village of Derrynoose in County Armagh, Ireland.

By late morning, they looked across some farm fields and saw the village in the distance. At the crossroad was a faded sign, "Doire Núis," with an arrow to the right. David had a feeling that this might be another right place, as the name in Irish meant oakwood of new milk.

Along the road to the village, they saw many farms, most were smaller than those in Baile Thormaid.

The fields were planted with many crops that they did not know and would soon enough learn were oats, barley, and flax. They were happy to see that every farm had at least one large field of potatoes; they continued into the village center.

All the way on their journey that morning, David kept thinking of how Connor and his wife acquired their farm.

It was Connor's parent's farm. They worked on it until they died; then, he inherited it.

David's mind was working. He secretly hoped to find an old couple with land, a couple who owned and were not tenant farmers, a couple with no heirs, a couple that needed help, his help. He would provide the help they needed, hopefully, befriend them, and maybe, just maybe, he could acquire the property when they died. He did not know how this would happen, but he believed it could. He did not share these thoughts with Catherine, as he was sure she would again take him to task for this selfish plan.

As they did in Baile Thormaid, the first stopping place would be the local church.

It was midday as they entered the village of Doire Núis. They passed the ruins of what must have been a century-old stone church. Closer to the village center, they passed thatched roofed stone cottages, and near the village center, they saw a small wooden church with a wooden cross above the front gable.

All the signs were written in Irish. From their training at the church school in Baile Thormaid, they quickly learned to read, write, and speak Irish, albeit with a Scottish accent.

David, Catherine, and Luke went to the front door. It was open, but no one was there.

"Hello," David said in a loud voice. No one answered.

They went outside and walked behind the church. A man was working cutting weeds around the church. David approached him. "Is the pastor about?" David inquired.

"Ya mean d' vicar, do ya?"

"I suppose I do," David responded.

"This be a Catholic church here. D'vicar lives in the vicarage. Just there," he said, pointing to the large house next to the church on the side road.

"Thank ya kindly. We'll see if we can find him," David said.

The vicarage was not like pastor Gregor's house; it was much larger with a front porch. The vicar was sitting on a rocker on the front porch, reading what looked like a Bible or a prayer book.

"Aye, sir, may we speak with ya?"

The vicar noticed the heavy Scottish brogue but understood the somewhat broken Irish.

"Yes, you can. How can I help yas? I am Father McGregor. I'm the vicar of this church."

David introduced his wife and son and went on to tell of their journey from Scotland. He did not mention the wedding in Baile Thormaid or the real reason they left Scotland or the reason they left Baile Thormaid, only that times were not good in Scotland or in Baile Thormaid.

"We came here in the hopes of finding good work, a place to live, raise our family, and find a church to join."

"Well now, this is the church, the only one. Are yas Catholic?"

David and Catherine looked puzzled. "I'm not sure what ya mean," said David. "We went to the Church of Ireland in Baile Thormaid."

"Well now, ya not be Catholic, but with some lessons at the church school, ya can join this church. As for work, what kind are ya looking for?" asked the priest.

"I have done a lot of farming, and I am good at fix'n most anyt'ing, and Catherine is a dressmaker and seamstress."

"You won't have any trouble finding work here. Most all of it is farming, except for the grain mill. But until ya find that, you can stay in the extra room here in the vicarage."

"Thank ye so much, Father," said David, thinking he had such a strange first name, Father. It wasn't until they went to a church school to become Catholics that he learned Father was a title, not a first name.

Over the next few days, David visited some of the local farms. Most were small, growing one or two crops. They were all operated by tenant farmers who lived in cottages on the property, while the workers lived in shed-like outbuildings. That evening, David asked the vicar if there were any farms owned and operated by the farmer.

"Oh no, they all be tenant farmers with owners in England or Dublin," said the vicar.

"All of them?" David asked.

"That's right, all of 'em."

David's grand plan just went up in smoke.

CHAPTER 5

Denny's Farm
1779–1819

David woke up early in the morning just as the sun was rising and headed out on the very road they came in on yesterday, looking for what might be the right farm, one where he could get a job. The first three or four were very small, and then the next one on the left seemed just the right size and not that far from town. The sign nailed on the fence post by the narrow dirt roadway leading to the farmer's house read, "Denny's Farm." As he approached the stone farmhouse, he could see three men in the distance, working in a potato field, and there was a man working in the garden behind the house. As David approached him, the man looked up. David gave him a wave and said, "Top o' the morn'n, sir. Are you Mr. Denny?"

"Yes, I am, and who are you, lad?"

"My name is David McNally. My wife and I just came into town yesterday, and I'm needing work."

"Oh, so its work yer look'n for, now is it?"

"Yes, Mr. Denny, it is, sir. I'm a very good worker, and I can do just about anything."

"Oh, ya can now, can ya?"

"Yes, sir, I can."

Denny thought a bit and said, "Well now, come with me, and we'll go to the hay barn." The walk to the barn wasn't far. The wooden barn was quite old, sided with sun-bleached vertical boards, and roofed with overlapping planks. Denny pointed to the left front barn door that was hanging by a twisted top hinge, twisted due to the weight of the door. The bottom hinge had broken away from the rotted wood to which it was attached.

"So you say you can fix most anything. Can you fix that?" he said, pointing to the door.

Without any hesitancy, David said, "Sir, yes, I can."

"Well, I'll tell you what, if you can fix that, maybe we can find some work for you to do around here, and by the bye, do you know farm work? This is a farm ya' know."

"Yes, I do, Mr. Denny," said David, and he went on telling him of his work on Connor's farm and his farming work with his father in Scotland.

"Well, good then. Come in the barn with me, and I'll show you me toolshed." The barn smelled of the dry hay and straw which was overhanging the lofts on either end.

The toolshed had everything David would need to fix the door, including a sharp handsaw, a hammer, tins of nails of different sizes, and a blacksmith's anvil.

"I'm going back to work in my garden right now. I'll come back and see you in a couple of hours and see how you are do'n."

David went back to Denny's house, where he was still working in the garden. Denny looked up. "Do ya need anything to help you with the door?"

"No, sir. Mr. Denny, the door's fixed."

"Yer not jokin' now, are ya?"

"No, sir, it be fixed and properly. Come, have a look."

They walked to the barn. Denny said, "Well, Janey Mack [an expression in Irish meaning great surprise]! Will ya look'e there, will ya? That is some good job ya did, and ya know what, ya jus' got a job."

"Oh, thank ya, Mr. Denny."

"No need to thank me, lad. Ya proved yerself ya did. Can ya start just now? Oh, and by the way, ya can call me Denny, me first name. Me last is O'Shawnesse."

"Well, Denny, is there any lodging here on the farm?"

"Yes, back there in the fields," Denny said, pointing to a stone building with a thatched roof. "That's the workhouse. I have three workers here and with you making four. It's big enough for you all. I have an extra bed in the house for ya."

"There could be one problem. I have a wife and a young son," Denny replied.

"David, see'n what ya can do, I really need you to help here. The other men are young but are just farmhands. I will make this work for both of us. I will. You come to start work here right now and build you and yer family in addition to the workhouse. There's plenty of stones that have been cleared from the fields piled nearby the workhouse. You can work without pay till it's done, but I will give you potatoes and other food from my garden, and then, as soon as you get that done, you'll be on the wages. Don't you want to know your wages?" Denny said.

"Well, I suppose, but I'm sure you'll be fair."

"You'll be paid a sixpence a week, ten hours a day, plus you'll get two potatoes and two turnips for you and your family."

"That's good with me. Can I start on the work right now?"

"Yes. Let's take a walk to the workhouse and have a look, and then, I'll have you meet the other men."

Denny showed David where he could add the shed and the supply of rocks.

"There's also there's a pile of logs and planks you can have in the barn for your rafters, bed, chairs, and a table, and plenty of thatch in the barn loft."

When they got out near the potato field, three men were cultivating. Denny introduced David to the men.

"Thank you, Denny. I'll get started right now If I can."

Denny returned to work in his garden, and David worked until the sunset until he could see no more; then, he left the farm and returned to the vicarage.

When he arrived, Catherine said, "Oh, David, I was so worried when you were so late."

"Not to worry, Catherine. I've got good news. I've got a job, and we will have a cottage to stay in, in a few weeks." He went on to tell her all about Denny and his farm.

David worked for the next three weeks, in the pouring rain, constructing the stone addition and thatched roof. He also built a stone chimney and set a large slab of flat stone for a hearth; he built a bed, two chairs, and a table. His family was ready to move in.

Catherine was pregnant again but, in August, had a miscarriage. She had pains in her abdomen for weeks. After seeing the doctor in the village, she was told she could not have any more children.

It was 1804. David was forty-two, Catherine was forty; Luke was almost twenty-six and a full head taller than his father. Luke had his father's muscular build and fair complexion and his mother's red curly hair.

All of that next year, David's presence and his work on the farm proved to be invaluable to Denny. David introduced him to planting beets and turnips, filling him in on his early experience, working on the community farm with his father in Scotland. David explained why his father always told him it was important to have more than one crop in case of a crop failure, so with that, Denny used David's idea and planted one large field with beets and the other with turnips. These turned out to be good cash crops for the farm, and being so pleased, Denny doubled David's wages.

Just as his father met his mother, Luke met a beautiful young woman at the church school he attended. Her name was Ann Campbell. Ann was eighteen and looked a lot like his mother when she was her age, with long reddish hair and a fair complexion, with a scattering of freckles across her nose and cheeks. She had piercing green eyes.

Her family, like the McNallys, left Scotland about fifteen years ago, finding their way to Armagh County.

The Campbells were tenant farmers on a small neighboring farm where the primary cash crop was hemp along with raising some hogs.

Luke married Ann in the spring of 1804, and in January of 1805, she gave birth to a son. They named him Daniel David McNally, the first name after David's father back in Scotland. Again, life was good and prosperous. It was a happy life for all the McNally family.

Young Daniel was a happy, healthy child. He attended the Catholic church school, and in the afternoons, by the time he was ten, he worked at the family farm with his father. He loved working side by side with his father, Luke, who was a good teacher. The days were long from the crack of dawn until sunset. Luke's father, David, constantly set the example of hard work and persistence with never a complaint. The two of them were a great team. Luke was just coming into his physical prime, and David was a seasoned farmer, still possessing the strength of his youth.

The year was 1819. Luke was now forty-one, his father fifty-seven, and young Daniel fourteen. The farm was a huge financial success, and in spite of high rental rates for the land, large amounts were saved. As David always said, "My father taught me that I must save for that rainy day," and there was more than one of them looming in their unseen future.

While the men tended the farm, Ann had the same dressmaking talents as her mother-in-law, Catherine. Together, they made clothing for their families and sold clothing to other families on the farms and in the village. Life for the McNally family was almost too good to be true.

CHAPTER 6

1819–1844
Prosperity and Death

The McNallys regularly attended the Catholic church in Derrynoose, never missing a Sunday. Daniel, fourteen, was just finishing up church school, where he was more interested in the "girl's class," who studied in a different room; he was always sure to seek them out after class, as there was still a half-hour of the mass still going on when their lessons were over.

Daniel was fascinated by the redheads, two of them, both Scot girls, Ann Monahan, fourteen, and Mary Cunningham, thirteen; they were both flirts, and Daniel couldn't get enough of them nor them enough of him.

Daniel's favorite was Ann. She just had that extra sparkle in her personality. The Sunday flirting sessions soon turned into courting sessions when the children left the church school and started attending mass.

When Daniel was seventeen, he asked Ann to marry him, and she did. Three years after their marriage, she had a baby boy they named Charles John after her father back in Scotland. Charles was a late-term baby, nine and a half months. He was a very large baby, making the birth difficult.

The birth of the baby was not easy for Ann. It was a long labor, and the birth canal tore badly, causing severe bleeding. A local doctor came, but even with stitches, he could not control the bleeding nor the infection that later came upon her. She was able to nurse the child for only two days. She died a week later. She was only twenty-one.

Ann was buried in a shallow grave covered with rocks at the top of the hill overlooking the farm under a large oak tree.

Her death was so unexpected and so tragic. The family and the whole village mourned for several months.

During that time, there were several nursing mothers at the church who gladly provided their milk for baby Charles.

As Charles grew, he became very close to his grandmother, Catherine, as she regularly took him to church school.

Daniel tried to take Charles as a child in the fields with him, as his father Luke did with him. When he did, it was a disappointing experience. Charles was just not going to be a working farmer and never would be. Charles's effeminate demeanor depressed Daniel, especially since Charles was going to grow into a big young man. Daniel resigned himself to the fact that Charles was not at all like him and left him in the cottage with the women, where Charles preferred to be.

It was a Sunday afternoon in April of 1830 when Denny asked David to come to his cottage. Over the years, David and Ann had become very good friends with the O'Shawnesses.

"Aye, Denny, is there a problem?"

"Well, not really, but I need to talk to ya, David. Next spring, I will be giv'n up my farm lease. I'm get'n too old fer farm'n. I want to see if the McNallys would want to take over the farm lease. Would ya want to?"

"Well, yes, we would. I, too, am getting up in years, but Luke is only fifty-one and can handle things well into the future."

Denny arranged for David and Luke to meet the factor, who was the middleman between the tenant farmer and the landowner in Dublin. He was due for his annual visit to inspect the farm.

The O'Shawnesses had saved most of their profits from the farm, so in June of 1830, they moved to Dublin. They promised to keep in touch with the McNallys but never did, as neither could read or write very well. The day they left, David put a new sign up on the gate, "McNally Farm."

When the McNallys took over the land lease, they agreed to tenant an additional fifty acres from Denny's landlord; David moved the family onto that land, where he and Luke built a new and larger house for the entire family. The soil on the new acreage was rich and fertile since it had never been planted. They planted fields of beets and turnips as the main cash crop and also some cabbage.

Life was good, and the years went by with most days being much the same, except Sundays, and they were always the same.

It was almost two years since the McNallys took over the land lease and tenanted the additional five acres from Denny's landlord. Daniel, now twenty-seven, finally started going back to church again. He found out that his other favorite redhead, Mary, had married a friend of his, Peter Cunningham. He was happy for them and their son James.

Peter worked at the local gristmill, where they ground oats. When James was two, his father was killed in a freak accident at the mill. The entire village was devastated, and Mary, at the young age of thirty-seven, was a widow. Besides his sister Mary, Peter Cunningham was survived by his brother Patt who was also a good friend of the McNally family.

When Daniel heard of Peter's tragic death, he couldn't get it out of his mind, wondering how Mary was handling it, now alone with a child. At first, he thought, *I best just stay away*, but he couldn't get her out of his mind. While Ann, his departed wife, was the real stunner of the two, Daniel realized there was something even more than a physical attraction between him and Mary.

He started going back to church in the hopes of seeing her, and he did. Their friendship blossomed over the next several years; they would often spend Sunday afternoons with her son James. They took long walks in the woodlands that surrounded the village, and after a few of those walks, they realized they were in love; they both had a strong love for one another.

In 1833, they were married. Mary and her son James were warmly welcomed as part of the McNally family. James Cunningham adopted the McNally surname. He was confirmed as James Cunningham McNally.

Mary got along especially well with Catherine. They had the same dressmaking talents, and together, they made clothing for the family and for other families on the farm, as well as in the village, adding to the family income.

In December of 1833, Mary had another son. They named him Peter David, in honor of Mary's first husband and the middle name after his father. David knew Peter Cunningham very well. He was a good man, and he liked having his son named for him.

Peter and James were half-brothers, only three years apart but grew up together working on the farm. They were totally alike and much like their father, a man's man, a hard worker, smart, and a person with a wicked sense of humor. Charles, on the other hand, was the antithesis of Peter, James, and his father. He was shy, seemingly lazy, and, although having a large physique, was quite effeminate, so much so that other than church school, he was kept on the farm as much as possible, sheltering him from probable ridicule or perhaps worse. Homaighnéasachas (homosexuality) was not socially acceptable, and often, the person was persecuted by beatings or worse.

Charles had no interest in being with men. He was asexual in that regard. He had many redeeming qualities; he was very caring, kind, extremely intelligent, and read everything he could find to read.

Peter looked up to James, his older half-brother. Peter and James were the best of friends. James was, and acted as, Peter's big brother and remained in that role for Peter's entire life.

Father and sons worked side by side and talked as they worked in the fields.

Peter asked, "Father, why did you choose these crops? Why not more potatoes?"

"Well, son, your grandfather taught me to plant a variety of vegetables because you never knew when any one of them might have big problems or be eaten by pests. In some ways, vegetables are just like people, very healthy most of the time, and then they are taken by a surprising disease, drought, or a plague of insects. He called those times 'the rainy days.' I hope we never see them."

The family farm had two cows and, depending on the time of year, three or four hogs and eight or ten sheep, plus one horse. A large garden of potatoes and parsnips was planted in the family garden next to the house.

Daniel had learned well from his father to diversify his crops and to have livestock as well. Life was better than good, and the years went by with most days being much the same, except for the weather, and then there were the Sundays. They were always the same. Sunday was church and a time for visits with friends and rest, never work.

David's family lived and worked on the farm for almost thirty years. The farming was good, providing the family with food, lamb, pork, and milk, and income to pay the land rent with a lot left over that was saved. The money was put into tins and secured under the floor of the cottage next to the hearth.

Everyone got along well in the family, albeit sometimes, a few would have a heated exchange. Any disagreements were settled by David. He had the last word, and while it wasn't always liked, it was honored, and no grudges were held. Well, maybe there were, but they were not permitted to be expressed. David believed in loving each other and faith in the good Lord to which he entrusted his family's fate.

Shortly after Charles' eighteenth birthday, in the spring of 1843, he told his father he had to get out on his own and leave the farm.

"Father, thank you for providing for me all these years and for protecting me. I know I am different, but hiding here on the farm is not good for me. There are other things in the world, and I am big enough and strong enough to take care of myself now."

"So just what are ya think'n you want to do?"

"I want to go to a big city, like Dublin. I don't know what is there waiting for me, but I need to go and find out, and I ask your blessing."

Daniel's feelings about Charles' sexuality had waned over the years, and he was supportive of his son.

"For sure, son, for sure. I will give you a good amount to take with you to get you started. You are a smart young man, and you will succeed in whatever you do. When do you want to do this?"

"I was hoping the next time you take the wagon up to Mullingar. I could go then and take the barge to Dublin. Is a ticket very expensive?"

"The cost is not too dear but worth every penny. Ya don't want to take the road south, it's too long, and now there are robbers in the forests, just waiting for travelers on the stagecoach. I'll get ya a barge ticket. That will be in two weeks."

"Thank you, Father. I will write to you and Mother often."

All in all, it was a family bound by love and faith, almost too good to be true.

David sold his produce in the village, and at harvest time, he took crates of beets, turnips, parsnips, and cabbages up to Mullingar, where the barges traveled on the Queens Canal to Dublin and Shannon. The Queen's Canal had just started operating for its full length in 1804, and that alone boosted the farm's profits substantially, as they far-out produced what was consumed in the surrounding farms and village.

But with all this prosperity and the wonderful family life, it was too good to be true. Catherine became very ill, first thinking she just had a bad cold, then a fever and sore throat.

The British Parliament had established dispensaries in the cities and villages of Ireland to provide health care, medicine, and advice was given gratis to the poor, and one was in Derrynoose.

David went to the village, leaving Catherine with the others. He found the dispensary and told the doctor his wife was severely ill, too ill to travel to the dispensary. The doctor returned with David to their cottage.

Catherine was suffering from a sore throat, fever, swollen glands, and weakness. The doctor looked into Catherine's mouth; the back of her throat was coated with a thick gray coating that was blocking her airway. He told the family that Catherine had a bad case of consumption (tuberculosis) and that she best be moved to other quarters away from the family as it was highly contagious. There were no treatments or antibiotics available at that time.

David and Luke set up a bed in the old work shed and started a fire in the hearth to warm the space.

David thought back to the first time he sat by a warm hearth with Catherine in Glasgow over sixty years ago. The images were still fresh in his mind's eye.

Luke carried his mother, wrapped in woolen blankets, to the shed, some fifty meters away. He tended the fire day and night to keep the shed comfortable and helped his mother with the chamber pot and changing her blankets. The soiled ones he soaked in lye water and dried outside over a fire.

The extreme congestion quickly became much worse. Mary brought warm broth and bread to Catherine every day, but she was unable to swallow. She was wasting away.

It was December 1843, right before Christmas, late in the evening, when the McNally family walked from their cottage across the field to the shed to see Catherine.

The field was awash in light from the setting full moon, appearing much large and redder than usual behind the tree-lined horizon.

David stared at the moon. A strange feeling of gloom settled over him and spread into his very being. It gave him a chill, a chill much colder than the night's winter wind.

They were all carrying oil lanterns as they crossed the field, and as they entered the shed, the room brightened; when they came closer to Catherine's bed, they could see her face in the lantern light. She was dead at eighty.

David fell to his knees, and looking upward; he cried, "Why did ya take me love? Why? Why?" He cried in an uncontrollable, primal moan of grief.

Luke helped his father up, and the family walked back to their cottage. The moon had set; the field was dark, except for the light from their lanterns.

The next morning when David, Daniel, and Luke finished making the coffin, David made the trip to the village and asked the vicar if he could come to the burial that afternoon. The vicar was shocked to hear of Catherine's death.

"David, I know you are angry with our God for taking Catherine but try to trust in his will. It is difficult and sometimes impossible to understand these things. I know you will miss her dearly, and I will pray for you and your family."

It was an unusually cold winter for this part of Ireland, and because the ground was somewhat frozen, David sent Daniel with a pickax and shovel up the hill to open the grave.

The vicar stood at the head of the open grave and read a prayer from his prayer book, and then made the sign of the cross. "Ashes to ashes, dust to dust, may the soul of Catherine McNally rest in heaven, forever. Amen."

Luke and Daniel, followed by David and his wife Mary, James, and Peter, walked by the open grave, and each threw a handful of soil down onto the coffin.

The rest of the family and the pastor returned to the cottage while Luke and David stayed, filled the grave, and covered it with stones.

Catherine was buried in a shallow grave under the same large oak tree as Ann's grave on the hilltop overlooking the farm. The grave was marked with a simple wooden cross made of sticks.

While the family was still deeply grieving over Catherine's death, the grim reaper was still swinging his sickle of death. Once more, it found its mark. Luke came down with the consumption only two days after his mother's funeral. He died three weeks later. He probably contracted it when he carried his mother from the family cottage to the shed some weeks before.

There was another funeral and burial on the hilltop. He was laid to rest next to his mother.

A year later, almost to the day his wife Catherine Ann died, David died. After her death, his grief never stopped. It just kept getting worse. His love for her was so intense. Nothing could replace her. His very soul yearned to be with hers; he died of a broken heart.

And now, there were three graves on the hilltop overlooking the family farm.

CHAPTER 7

1844–1847
Escaping "An Gorta Mór"
The Great Starvation

U pon David's death, Daniel, at thirty-nine, assumed the patriarchal role in the family. James was fourteen and working full-time on the farm. Peter, eleven, was still in church school but helped in the early morning and late afternoon hours.

The family continued to go to church, where they had known the Cunninghams ever since the mill accident and the death of Patt Cunningham's brother Peter, James' father. The McNallys and Cunninghams became very good friends and usually spent Sunday afternoons at one of their farms, enjoying a late afternoon supper. Patt and Sarah Cunningham had one child, a daughter, Bridget, one year younger than Peter. They would play together like brother and sister.

While family life and local friendships thrived, this was a bad time to raise a family, a bad time to own a farm, and for that matter, a bad time to live anywhere in Ireland. By 1845, a potato blight spread like wildfire throughout the farms in Ireland, including the McNally farm and the neighboring farm tenanted by the Cunningham family. It was fortunate that the McNally farm had a diversification of crops as they lost their entire potato crop in the fall of 1845.

While they were surviving on the beets, parsnips, and turnips, they lacked a decent starch form in their diet. The Cunninghams suffered a worse plight at their farm. Theirs was strictly a potato farm. Daniel graciously provided the Cunningham family with his other root crops, meat, and milk. He saved their lives and the lives of other neighbors by doing so.

By 1847, most all tenant farms were repossessed by the wealthy landlords for lack of rent payment, and starvation followed by death was taking over the county.

When the blight hit his farm, Daniel reacted quickly. He harvested seedpods from the beets and turnips and planted all his fields with them after pulling and burning the remnants of the failed potato crop. He shared his seeds with Patt Cunningham.

For a while, the Irish were able to sell enough of the failing potato crops to meet their rent, but they were bringing in less and less. As time went by, people were not making enough of an income to buy anything, and the potatoes were all gone.

Daniel could see his lifetime savings going down for the first time with no foreseeable hope on the horizon. If it were not for his animals and other root crops, his family would have been on their way to starvation.

As 1847 closed, nearly a million Irish had perished from starvation. The population suffered first from the blight, then poverty, then eviction, followed by hunger and, inevitably, death.

Daniel and Mary knew if they stayed in Derrynoose much longer, they would be evicted from their farm and, in months, if not sooner, would be in a state of starvation and facing death. They had money, but there was no food to buy. There were oats but no wheat in Derrynoose; hence, no bread, and the locals did not eat oats. It made them sick.

Daniel had saved the farm profits for years and kept the money in tins buried under the floor of the cottage. Daniel spoke with Mary, James, and Peter, and they decided they needed to get out of Derrynoose, out of County Armagh, and move to Dublin, where they might have a better chance of survival. They had been receiving letters from Charles in Dublin, where they sensed they would have a better chance of surviving. Mary spoke with the children about their plan and asked them to remain faithful to God and their father.

They continued to attend church, which besides a place to worship, was a place to get all the latest news. Daniel met his friend, Patt Cunningham, and told him of their planned departure.

"Well, I'll tell ya, Daniel, Sarah, and I have the same plan. We've told our daughter, Bridget, about the move. She seemed a bit worried about the uncertainty. Well, we are too, but we must trust the Lord. We're go'n to Dublin and plan to leave in a week. The three of us will be on the canal barge from Mullingar next Monday. If I di'na see you today, I was go'n out to your farm to let ya know. Will ya be leav'n soon, will ya?"

"We'll be on a barge one week after you leave. That would be April 10. We need to arrange to meet up with you in Dublin. I'm not sure of the exact date we will arrive, so can we say we will meet at the Dublin barge dock on the first Sunday of next month at noon?"

"Yes, we'll plan to be there."

"Good. When we arrive, we will look for a place to live. Charles has sent us a city map with some possible places, so hopefully, when we meet up with you, we will be settled in."

The men shook hands and wished each other well on their travels then gathered their families together and started packing for the move.

They just took their clothing, money, and a sack of beets, turnips, and carrots. The barge would provide drinking water.

The day before Daniel decided to leave the farm, he went to the top of the hill to his family's graves.

The stone-covered graves surrounding the giant oak tree were grown over with grasses, and between the graves, a small oak tree had grown over the years from the falling acorns. He knew the roots would entwine the gravesites, and it was God's way to protect the graves in the event the British found them and tried to desecrate them. He said a prayer, then threw what remained of the crosses marking the graves into the woods and returned to the work at hand at his cottage.

Daniel, Mary, James, and Peter, prepared for their departure from their farm.

The day before their departure, Daniel walked into the village to see the vicar.

He told him of their plans to leave their farm behind and go to Dublin. "Anything at the farm is at your disposal, Father. There are still vegetables in the fields, and the sheep and goats can feed the village people as well. I'm sure you can get some folks to help you manage that."

"Thank you, Daniel. Your generosity will probably save our people, at least some of them, at least for a while. God bless you and your family."

On April 10, 1847, the McNally family started their move, a move from poverty and the threat of death, to Dublin, where they would find poverty but also life.

They packed the one-horse cart and began their day-long journey on the Keady Road, forty-nine kilometers to Mullingar and the Queen's Canal.

The Queen's Canal construction started in 1757. It was completed in 1804, taking forty-seven years, covering a distance of one hundred forty-five kilometers from the River Liffey in Dublin across Ireland, tying into the upper reaches of the River Shannon.

Travel on the barge was somewhat expensive for the McNallys, but it avoided the long stagecoach ride, which was often fraught with robberies and very poor road conditions along the way.

Daniel's plan was to sell the horse and cart after arriving in Mullingar to someone, even if for a pittance. They had to leave it behind.

Daniel went into the ticketing office and asked the ticket clerk if he might be interested in buying his horse and cart.

"Well, now, why should I buy it if you are going one way to Dublin? You can't take it with you. It seems it will just be abandoned property, free for the taking, now doesn't it?"

Daniel was quick to answer, "Why, no. No, not at all. If you won't give me a fair price for my horse and wagon, I would rather give them away to a local farmer here in town, so can we do business?"

The clerk thought for a moment and said, "I'll tell you what, I will give you the tickets in exchange for the horse and wagon. Is that fair?"

"It's not really fair, but I will agree to it, as I can use the saved ticket money for better things."

The trip down the canal for the McNally family was uneventful but slow. The barge carried both cargo and passengers and moved at a slow three kilometers per hour, pulled by a horse on the adjacent towpath. The horses were changed from time to time at various lock locations.

Each evening, the barge would tie up for the night at a lock. Daniel sent Peter and James off to bring back some firewood while Mary cut up some turnips and beets, including the leafy tops. The barge had several oil lamps to light the decks by night, and those flames were used to start the cooking fires. The menu never changed but was both nutritious and muddy in taste. No one outwardly complained about anything, but their thoughts were filled with fear and doubt. They were thankful to be alive.

The barge had to pass through forty-six locks from the high point at Mullingar to the sea lock in Dublin, where the canal connects to the River Liffey at Dublin Harbor. Right before the river lock was the four-span stone, arched Leinster Aqueduct that went over the River Liffey. All the passengers were amazed to see the barge in the canal bridging this tributary of the River Liffey below.

The journey was seventy-seven kilometers and took six days to Dublin City.

Daniel hoped he could find some decent and inexpensive food besides the beets and parsnips they had been eating all week; they all had bright purple stains around their mouths, and their teeth were stained purple too, a funny sight to behold, looking much like a pantomime troupe from a repertory company.

Daniel was confident that he and his family would not starve, and that in Dublin, he would find some kind of good work. He was sure they would survive. They had to. He would make sure they did.

Daniel was careful to keep track of the days, for, in less than two weeks, they were to meet up with the Cunninghams and their son Charles at the barge pier on the river.

They had been corresponding with Charles on a regular basis, so he was aware of the meeting time and place.

At last, the barge passed through the last lock, which opened into the River Liffey and the Dublin City harbor.

The McNallys were amazed. They had never seen a city before. Large three and four-story stone buildings surrounded the port, and beyond that, towering church spires. James carried the heavier sacks, and Peter and Mary carried the rest.

They crossed the Liffey and walked north along the western quay to Dock Quay. James had his eye on the towering church spire. It was only a short walk, and they were there. The sign in front read, "Christ Church Cathedral."

There was a smaller front door that was not locked. They entered and could not believe the beauty of this place; towering arched columns and beautiful stained-glass windows lined both sidewalls. It was quiet except for the sound of feet shuffling over the stone floor ahead of them to the left in the adjoining nave and then the sound of a heavy door closing with an echo, then silence.

They were at the rear of the cathedral, sitting on the last bench, when Daniel said, "Let's just sit here a moment and say a prayer of thanks for our deliverance to this place."

After praying, they walked up the center aisle, taking in all there was to see, and after a brief stop at the altar, they went back down the aisle and out the same door they came in.

Upon exiting, they saw a funeral interment already underway in the adjoining churchyard. The procession must have just been leaving the church when they were entering.

The sight of this instantly brought back the remembrance of their own family losses. They stood at a distance and watched and listened. The sound of the handfuls of soil thrown onto the casket was all too familiar.

Daniel wanted to speak with the priest after the service was over, so he whispered to the others to be quiet and patient.

When the family left, the priest noticed the McNallys standing near the front corner of the cathedral, and he approached them.

"Good day, my friends. Can I help you?"

"Yes, Father, perhaps you can. We just arrived by barge this morning. We need some food and need to find a place to stay," said Daniel.

"Well now, not far from here, you will find a free soup kitchen. You can get a good hot meal there and meet others in your situation. They will be better able to guide you. It's called 'Soyer's Soup Kitchen' at a place called 'Croppies Acre,' just up there," he said, pointing up the adjoining street. "It's in a large tent. You can't miss it."

"Thank you, Father, and God bless you."

The walk was worth it. They found the tent and quickly learned where the end of the line was. Every so often, a bell rang, and another hundred people were let in while others exited.

While they waited their turn, they met John McNeil, a single man who made a similar trip several weeks ago from a farm north of Dublin. John told them they could follow him to the neighborhood where he found decent housing for a reasonable rent.

After they finished their bowls of a hearty meat and vegetable soup with bread, John led them to a poor residential area where he lived. It wasn't the best nor the worst either.

Daniel found a two-room second-floor tenement that would be sufficient. Unknown to him at the time was the fact that it was very close to a tannery, which, when the wind shifted, blew its acrid smells often for days on end into their living quarters. Closed windows could not keep the smell out.

Daniel asked about work in the city and found that as a farmer, there was not much available except as a common laborer. He was desperate for work.

James, at sixteen, was young and strong and found a job working for the city on road maintenance. Together, his wages and his father's would pay the rent with a modest amount left for simple foodstuffs. Peter, at thirteen, was still in church school.

It wasn't much, but in the past two weeks, they found a place to live and work to keep them alive.

Daniel checked the date. Tomorrow they were to meet their son Charles and the Cunninghams.

"Mary, tomorrow is the big day. Are you excited?"

"Yes, Daniel, I am, extremely so. I can't imagine how Charles must have grown. His letters to us have been so encouraging. I think I shall have trouble sleeping tonight just thinking about tomorrow."

"Let's get some sleep, Mary. It will be a busy day tomorrow."

CHAPTER 8

1847
Dublin to America

I t was a sunny morning, the first Sunday of May 1847. The McNallys just left mass at the small Catholic church near their tenement. They walked toward the harbor to meet their son, Charles, and the Cunninghams as planned. They got to the barge pier just as the noon church bells rang. The pier was empty except for two lock workers and a few people strolling along the Northern Quay.

They were especially excited about seeing Charles, whom they had been writing to since he left home in Derrynoose four years before. He had written to them about the great job he had working with a Scot who owned a spirits business importing and selling whiskey. Right after they arrived at the meeting place, Charles came running down the quay.

"Mother, Father!" he hollered as he ran. Charles was a grown man now at twenty-two. Since he left the farm, he had grown several inches in height and put on a few pounds. All the McNallys jumped for joy at the sight of him. He was a sight to see in "city clothes," much more fashionable than even the Sunday clothing of Derrynoose.

Daniel, Mary, James, and Peter all enjoyed the reunion. They asked Charles all sorts of questions about Dublin and his life there.

Charles, while now appearing only slightly effeminate, had grown into a tall, muscular, handsome man, which dominated his appearance. No one would dare question his manhood.

Charles wrote to his family regularly, so he knew of the deaths and famine problems in Derrynoose and the rest of the country. They knew he had a good job, one that paid well and one he liked, one where he was able to save a lot of what he made.

His father trained him well in being both responsible and penurious. Although penurious with his saving and careful with his spending, he was equally as generous with others. Daniel was proud to hear firsthand of his son's success.

Charles read a lot and was a self-educated man. He did not work on Saturday or Sunday. He respected Sunday as the Lord's day and attended mass and rested, usually reading at home. Saturdays were spent at the library in Trinity College, reading history and English literature. He had become both a very astute scholar and a successful businessman.

They kept looking for the Cunninghams and continued to wait for some time, feeling something must have gone wrong. Finally, as it was going on twelve-thirty, they saw Patt and Sarah walking down the quay, along with Bridget. When they spotted each other, both families ran toward each other.

Daniel and Patt met with a hearty handshake. Mary and Sarah hugged, and Peter and Bridget embraced, so excited to be reunited.

Next to the barge pier was a public park with trees, pathways, and benches. Patt had stopped at a bakery shop and bought a large loaf of bread and some sweet cakes to welcome his friends.

They broke bread together. Daniel said a prayer and thanked the Lord for their deliverance. They all shared stories of their days since leaving Derrynoose, and the Cunninghams and Charles told of their experiences in Dublin.

As they crossed the river, Patt Cunningham took the group on a tour of the neighborhoods near the Dublin harbor. Patt asked Daniel, "How did you manage to get housing here?"

"Well, we found a place we could afford but not the best of neighborhoods. It will have to do for a while. It's not far from here. Let's all go there so you can have a look, and then we would like to see where you and Charles live."

They all went, including Charles and Patt, who then showed them where they lived and the churches they attended. The room Patt and Sarah found was in a better part of the neighborhood yet close enough that the families all met every Sunday at the same church.

Charles found an apartment closer to the business district with a short walk to the spirit shop and not far from a Catholic Cathedral.

Patt told them that it wasn't long after he arrived in Dublin that he was able to find work at the Jamesons whisky distillery. He explained it was a matter of being at the right place at the right time. Jamesons had just decided to open their own cooperage, which was a skill he learned as a young man while working at the mill in Derrynoose. As a job applicant, he had a lot going for him. First, he slept at the "hiring" door and was the first one in line. He was thirty-seven years old, strong, and handsome, and he was able to demonstrate his skill as a cooper, and better than all the other reasons, he was Catholic. He was hired and was paid two and a half shillings a day, almost three times that of a common laborer.

Daniel had trouble finding a job. He was a farmer, and he was in a city. After over a week of trying, he saw a sign on the tannery, "Help Wanted, no experience needed."

He got the job. It was hellish work. Work for Daniel at the tannery was dismal, long hard hours in an atmosphere of heat, acids, and other acerbic chemicals.

Daniel's job at the tannery as a Moroccan finisher didn't require much training. It was simply filthy work, a job nobody wanted, but times were not good in Ireland.

The tanning process for goatskins was called Morocco finishing. It began with liming the raw skins to partially remove the skin fat and grease. Hairs were then picked off as much as possible. The skins were scraped and then treated in a series of baths with poisonous substances, including cyanides, arsenic sulfides, and other toxic compounds.

The final goatskin leather product was sold to bookbinders to produce top-quality leather-bound books. The tannery owners got good profits, except for the pittance they paid their workers, one shilling a day. It was not much, but it would buy two loaves of bread.

Daniel tried very hard to save as much of his family's wages as he could. He grew up learning from his father that you had to save for the "bad times," and it was good he did, for these times in Dublin were indeed "bad times."

James had acquired a job as a common laborer working with a city road crew. The pay was one shilling a day, and Peter was taken out of school to join his father working at the tannery, where his one shilling a day was added to the pot.

Bridget worked with her mother, Sarah, making clothing, some for her family and some for sale.

She loved to spend her free time on Sunday afternoons with Peter. Usually, they would leave the neighborhood and just explore the city together. Peter also had a special fondness for Bridget.

During their time in Dublin, Patt gave Daniel a little extra money to help his family, which Daniel humbly accepted and promised someday to return every penny; that day never came.

After Patt worked for six months, the management spoke to the men in the cooperage department. They were looking for employee recommendations for both experienced coopers and potential apprentices. They were going to expand the cooperage operations to meet the needs of their growing sales. Hiring off the street was not working. Many of the men, while experienced coopers, were drunks and troublemakers on the job. The management would trust the moral judgment of their proven employees.

Patt at once thought of James McNally, whom he knew was smart, a hard worker, and whom he knew could learn this trade. He also knew that James was wasting his time on the city road crew. James was interviewed and was hired; he worked side by side with Patt, learning the cooperage trade.

Over the next two years, most days were the same, just like at the farm, except for Sundays, and they, too, were all the same. While the Cunninghams were doing all right, they just had their heads above water, what with helping the McNallys.

Daniel's family was doing all right as well. They had saved some money, but it was not the best of times. They could not see a prosperous future as Dublin was overcrowded, and the overall economy was bad and getting worse by the day. People were starving in the streets.

In the spring of 1850, at their usual after-church get-together, Daniel and Patt had a serious discussion about their plights, about their family's futures. Something had to change. There was much talk on the streets about immigration, immigration to America. Ireland was moving to America.

Daniel and Patt talked about this for several weeks. Patt and his wife were in great health and felt confident they could survive the arduous trip, but Daniel's health was, at best, just okay. He knew he probably would not be able to survive the trip to America, so with that David spoke with his oldest son, Charles, telling him of the family plans.

Charles told his father and stepmother that he was not interested in going to America and that in spite of the famine and hard times, he was doing better than most. He also told his parents that they were more than welcome to stay with him, where he would take care of them in their old age and provide for them. Daniel and Mary decided it was best for them to stay in Dublin with Charles.

So it was decided, just as thousands of the Irish did, that the McNallys and Cunninghams were moving to America. That is, all except Daniel, his wife Mary, and Charles. And with that, James, now nineteen, took his father's place as the man of the house.

Daniel kept a share of the McNally money for himself, and the rest was pooled with Patt's. Combined, they jointly had ample money to sail to America.

At that time, most Irish immigrants did not travel in family units because of the cost. The McNallys and Cunninghams were fortunate they saved and now were traveling as a family unit.

James and Patt checked the shipping companies going to America. There were many as it seemed all of Ireland was in a rush to get there. After a few days of shopping for tickets and asking a lot of questions to the ticket vendors, they decided on a three-masted ship called a British packet, the *Dylan*, an Irish name meaning "ray of hope." It sailed to New York from Liverpool. The contract ticket included the Irish Sea crossing to Liverpool from Dublin Harbor on a slightly smaller schooner, the *Barbara*.

The alternate would have been passage on a steamer, which was much faster, with better accommodations, but the cost was much more, more than they could afford.

Wooden-hulled side-wheel steamers were three-masted sailing packets. They started regularly scheduled voyages from Liverpool to New York and were much faster than the sailing ship without steam power. They could cruise at nineteen knots, making the Atlantic crossing in less than six days.

This was not an option for the McNallys and Cunninghams. They opted on a sailing schooner that would make the trip from Liverpool to New York, taking anywhere between six to fourteen weeks, depending on the weather, possible adverse winds, and currents; the course of the *Dylan* was destined to encounter all of these.

The families purchased their ticket contracts, which included an overnight sail from Dublin to Liverpool, then transferring to the three-masted packet to New York. And so it was. The plan was set to leave Dublin and its problems behind and go to America for a new life with a brighter future.

The next week, on a Monday morning, the families gathered their possessions, which were few, bundled them up, and headed for the Dublin Harbor. Moving was not new to them, except this one seemed exciting and much more hopeful.

They had all said their goodbyes and bon voyages the night before, knowing it would be an even sadder occasion when the ship set sail. They agreed to write often and keep up on any family news.

When the McNally-Cunningham families arrived at the dock, their ship was buzzing with activity. Workmen were loading barrels, crates, and other cargoes, and over a hundred passengers were milling around on the dock, waiting to board.

At about nine o'clock, the ship's clerk shouted from the gangway, "We will commence boarding! Have your contract ticket ready! We will begin with the steerage class! All aboard, please!"

The order of boarding started with the worst class, steerage, the lowest level on the ship. These passengers would have to be checked in and go to their quarters first. Next, the second class, and finally, the first class. The first-class boarding last gave them the least time below the top deck and more time in the fresh air.

The second-class passengers were called to board. When all were on board, the clerk shouted, "Roll call, roll call! Quiet, please." After which, he read off the family names. "When ye hear yer name, come here with yer contract ticket." He proceeded to read the names and finally said, "The McNally and Cunningham families, traveling as a family unit, step forward, please."

James and Patt went and presented their family tickets. The clerk said, "That's five second-class fares. Ya can go down one deck to your quarters."

The passengers stayed huddled, listening to the rest of the second class roll call. Meanwhile, crew members were searching every possible hiding place for stowaways. They found one hiding in an empty crate. He was bound and taken off the ship to be delivered to the local magistrate for prosecution. He would probably spend several years in prison with hard labor.

Patt and James lead their group one deck below to their quarters. Second-class was a dimly lit space with one oil lamp hanging from the overhead. The ports, or vents, to the outside were open, and they could feel the fresh air coming in but not enough to overpower the stench of urine, feces, and vomit from previous trips that were never bothered to be scrubbed clean. Bunk beds were three high on each side of the ship. They stowed their belongings on hooks and ropes to the overhead. All they had was a change of farm clothes, Sunday clothes, and an extra pair of shoes, plus a blanket for each person. They waited till the first-class passengers were in their quarters, one deck above, in much better conditions, and then retreated to the open deck for fresh air and to watch the departure from the harbor. They all watched until Ireland slipped away in the midst of the day.

The overnight sail to Liverpool was uneventful, and the sea was calm. Once there, they disembarked and carried their belongings to the *Dylan*, which was docked a short distance away. The boarding procedures were the same, and they set sail at ten in the morning.

The *Dylan* was not as bad as the infamous "coffin ships," ships that were in great disrepair, where the owners packed in as many souls as they could to get the most money. There was no concern for their health or safety or even their lives. Coffin ships often lost more than fifty percent of their passengers before reaching America. The owners didn't care to the point they would rather the passengers die so there would be fewer mouths to feed. The *Dylan* was just a few notches above a "coffin ship" standard. Food was porridge and hard biscuits, which were spotted with mold. Drinking water was rainwater collected in barrels. It had a distinct taste of cheap whiskey that came from the dregs of the whiskey that was left in the barrels. At least it was germ-free.

The first three days offered calm seas and steady breezes as the *Dylan* made a steady nineteen knots into what seemed like fair weather. On day four, before sunrise, Peter was on deck enjoying the fresh ocean air. He breathed it in with a prayer of thanks. Soon after dawn broke, the eastern sky got brighter and brighter, turning to a bright red just before the sunrise. Peter understood the meaning of a red sky in the morning, "A sailor's warning." While he did not understand the science of it, that the sun's rays were going through a high-pressure ridge, a thicker layer of atmosphere that filtered out the blue spectrum, leaving only the visible red, he, nonetheless, knew they were in for some bad weather and soon. He went below and told James and Patt they would probably be in for some rough seas ahead.

Sure enough, that evening, the seas began to get rough, with peaked waves, white caps, and ocean spray from the bow wake, keeping the decks a-washed. The sky was filled with low dark clouds as a heavy, steady rain fell. In the middle of the night, the sea became tumultuous in the gale. The ship pitched and rolled violently, waking everyone.

James, in spite of his young age, at seventeen, was always a leader. He told everyone in second-class to remain in their bunks and to pray for their deliverance from the storm. The gale continued for three days. No one left their quarters, and there was nothing to eat, nor did anyone want to eat. All the passengers were seasick, and four died, not from the storm but from diseases that were brought on board in Dublin and persisted in spreading death throughout the ship. On average, one person died each day on this voyage, a total of twenty souls.

Every day the sanitary conditions on the ship became worse. Diseases were running rampant, and so were head lice. James, Peter, Patt, and two other men in second-class kept the deck cleaned by mopping up the vomit when it happened. Every other day, both Patt and James insisted that everyone in second class would go on deck, strip down, and bathe with ocean water and lye soap, telling them if they didn't, they would die of the disease. There was no room for vanity. Always thinking ahead, James had packed six bars of lye soap. He tied a rope to their clothing, making a string of clothes. He dropped it into the ocean, pulled the line up on the deck, and scrubbed each item with soap before returning the line to the sea for a final rinse. After half an hour, he pulled in the line and strung it from the mast to a ratline at the gunwale for it to wave in the breeze and dry out.

Almost every day, depending on the seas and weather, one person was committed to the deep, dead from smallpox, typhoid fever, typhus, scarlet fever, tuberculosis, pneumonia, meningitis, dysentery, diphtheria, or rheumatic fever. The dead were all passengers from steerage in the depth of the ship. The body was weighted down with a ballast block tied to their chest, covered with a linen sheet, and placed on a board that was placed in the gangway, extending to the sea. The captain would routinely hold one of the shortest funerals in history. He would stand by the corpse and say, "I hereby commit your soul to God and the deep." After which, a sailor would raise the ship-side end of the plank, sliding the body to the sea. This was a daily event most days for sixteen weeks.

By the time they reached the entrance of New York harbor, over one hundred souls had died, nearly a quarter of the embarking passengers. The McNallys and the Cunninghams survived the trip, thanks to James's persistence, faith, and leadership and with Patt and Peter's help.

Right before the ship entered the Hudson River, the entrance to New York harbor, there were two more dead in steerage from smallpox. The captain knew the corpses would not be allowed to be off-loaded in New York, so he quickly disposed of them at sea without the usual funeral.

The ship sailed up the Hudson River, and after passing Fort Jay (a star-shaped fort on Governor's Island in New York harbor named for the New York Governor and Supreme Court Justice) on the right, they were met by a steam tug that did the final pushing and maneuvering. The sails were furled as the *Dylan* was eased into the dock amid an endless line of ships. All on board were filled with excitement at seeing America, their saving place, at last, they thought.

The captain had prepared the disembarkment papers for all passengers, listing the names, ages, and port of departure, along with a list of those who died at sea.

After the ship was secured at the dock on the western side of the Battery, the ship's clerk ordered the disembarkation. "First-class passengers first. Giv'em room. Step back."

All the ships were so close together that planks could span the space between opposing gangways, from which a gangplank sloped down to the dock.

The clerk called for the disembarkation of the second-class passengers. At last, the McNally's and Cunningham's feet stepped onto American soil.

CHAPTER 9

1847–1848
New York City

When the McNallys and Cunninghams disembarked, they were part of a sea of huddling masses. Hundreds of them were fenced in by a thirteen-foot fence to the East and the Hudson River on the West.

They moved from there to another fenced-in area, like so many cattle. First, there was a medical check. The doctors, all wearing surgical masks, hats, and gloves, looked into their eyes, mouth, and ears and felt their heads. If healthy, they were signed in as and given an alien paper form to register. Anyone with suspect symptoms was sent back on their ship, where likely they would die on the return trip.

This crush of humanity slowly shuffled south toward a narrow gate to a large round building that jutted out into the river. As they got closer, they could read the sign over the entrance doors, "Castle Garden."

Initially, Castle Garden was built as a fort to protect the harbor, then after the war of 1812, it was converted into a theatre venue. In 1820, Castle Garden started accepting immigrants, and in 1822, the State of New York's Board of Emigration Commissioners established it as the "Emigrant Landing Depot at Castle Garden."[1]

---

[1] Castle Garden Museum.

When they entered the building, it was the only building they had been in that was clean other than a church, and while the immigration process was hectic; it was organized. They exited the building hours later.

They followed the crowd toward the open gates with the sign overhead, "WELCOME TO THE UNITED STATES OF AMERICA."

Many dropped to their knees and kissed the ground again as they did when they stepped off the gangplank.

The McNallys and Cunninghams split off from the crowd that was walking straight to the north. They continued a bit to the east and then walked north along the East River. Patt and James led the way. James, in particular, always seemed to lead by sheer instinct; that was what directed most of his days.

The scene was not looking inviting. The street was as fifthly as the Dublin wharves. Many of the buildings were boarded shut, and those that were advertising for help had signs, "NO IRISH NEED APPLY." This was not the image of America they had imagined.

The crowds of people all were speaking in many languages. They were able to hear over the din a lot of Irish and English, which seemed somewhat reassuring. While they were grateful they arrived safely and alive, maybe because of their exhaustion and the trauma of the trip, they did not see anything much different from Dublin; actually, the first impression was worse than Dublin.

As they walked north along the river street, a group of four people was approaching, heading south. As they got within earshot, they could hear they were speaking in Irish. As they got closer, James spoke in a loud voice, "A chairde maidin mhaith, Conas atá tú?" It was Irish for "Good morning, friends. How are you?"

They all continued to speak in Irish. James asked if there was an Irish section of the city.

"You couldn't have gotten closer," one of them replied. "Just up a few blocks to the left is Five Corners. There's a lot of Irish there. Keep walking, and you will see an Irish pub on the corner. You will feel at home there. We're sure."

They walked a little further, and there it was, like an oasis in the desert, the sign. The pub read, "O'Connor's Irish Pub," in gold letters on a light green background with dark green shamrocks at either end.

Speaking to James, Patt said, "Well, my friend, after that sixteen-week voyage, I be think'n we just got to heaven."

They went through the front door, and the barroom was alive. There were fellow Irishman everywhere, men at the bar drinking Guinness, and groups of women sitting at tables talking. Everyone was talking, a wonderful cacophony and melody the soul sorely needed.

There were children crawling around on the floor, laughing, and playing, with men talking and drinking at the bar. All in all, a happy, intoxicating elixir, much overdue.

Bridget and Sarah joined a table of three other women and introduced themselves. Patt, James, and Peter stood behind the men at the bar listening to the jabbering.

When the conversations had a lull, Peter spoke up, "We just got off the boat. Where can we find housing with Irish cairde?" It was Irish for "friends."

One of the men said, "You're at the right place. We all live in Five Corners, just out front and to the right a few blocks. It's a bit crowded, but the rents are decent, and we all look out for each other."

"Ya know, a lot in this city don't particularly like us Irish. It's our Catholic religion they hate. They do hate it and us. Something must be wrong with them, don't ya think?" the stranger said with somewhat of a laugh. They all joined in with laughter and ordered another round of Guinness.

Patt ordered some soup, bread, and water for the women. The men had Guinness, which was like a wonderful dark brown wine from heaven, topped with foamy, bitter-tasting clouds.

They finished the meal, the first real food they had in four months, left the pub, and headed to Five Corners.

Five Corners was named because of the five streets that formed an intersection on the lower east side of Manhattan Island. It was primarily an Irish and Jewish ghetto, crowded, filthy, filled with crime and prostitution, but it was in America.

There was no famine, and the floors of the apartments were wood, not dirt.

The apartments had real ceilings, not thatch that leaked in the rains and weather. They had cast iron stoves with chimney pipes, not smoke holes in the thatch. This was their new home.

The men found suitable housing for the night, small and cramped but suitable. They paid to squeeze into the basement of another Irish family's one-room tenement. It was cold and wet, but this had to be the starting point.

In the morning, James and Patt set out their plans for the day. Patt said he was going to look beyond Five Points as he could afford a better place and neighborhood. James decided to find a place in Five Points, at least for a while, to save money, and until he and Peter could find work, they had to find decent-paying jobs to build up the family war chest, but for now, they found a small room. They slept on the floor on their spread out bundles of clothes, covered themselves with blankets, and fell asleep. It was their second night in America.

Patt had more money left after the voyage for a place with a higher rent, as it was only he, Sarah, and Bridget he had to provide for, and after seeing Five Corners and having told James that he would find a better place, he did, a bit to the south and west.

James and Peter stayed in Five Corners living in these poor conditions for almost a year, trying to build up a nest egg.

James had no trouble in getting a job at a nearby cooperage where Patt Cunningham also secured employment.

They both learned this trade in Ireland. The only job Peter could get in the area was as a Morocco finisher at a tannery. There was a whole section near Five Corners called "The Tannery," where both small and large tanneries were located. Peter dreaded the work, but it was work, work he knew; he toughed it out.

James didn't want to risk disease or any harm to himself or Peter and could no longer tolerate living in these conditions. He had been frugal managing both his and Peter's earnings, securing the money in a tin under the floorboards of their humble abode.

They now had enough money saved to upgrade their conditions. Peter also was sure he had to leave the job at the tannery as it was adversely affecting his health; he would get another job, any job, anything but a Morocco finisher, but what?

Bridget and her mother, Sarah Cunningham, worked, making clothing for the men and for themselves; they worked very well together and were all good friends.

Peter and Patt Cunningham became the best of friends; Patt was like an uncle to James and Peter.

Peter discussed his work situation, hours on end with Patt after church on Sundays. Patt was smart and had a good sense of what was going on in the city, especially in the job market.

"Peter, you know, you have many talents, and you are smart. You learned in your farming years with your father. You must think of the things you could do but most importantly, the things you liked to do the most. Then you will find that one thing you really like and do well, and you will be paid well to do it."

Peter, while thinking himself a born leader, often led in the wrong direction, but he respected Patt's wisdom.

"Patt, thanks for the encouragement. I will put my mind to it," he said, and he did.

He thought about what he liked to do the most on the farm. He was not just a good farmer. He was good with his hands, good with building things like wooden tables, chairs, and making doors. While it never dawned on him that he was an expert carpenter, he had the God-given gift of this skill. He knew he still had those talents, and just now, he finally recognized them. With this new insight, he began speaking to those at church who worked in that trade.

It wasn't long until he found work at the Obrien and Walsh Furniture Company, located only a few blocks from St. Andrews, their church.

The church was their lifeline to faith and friends, and they loved the parish priest, Father Luke.

Father Luke Evers initiated the "Printers' Mass," held at two thirty on Sunday morning, which allowed Catholic workers at nearby Printing House Square, where *The Sun*, *The New York*

Telegram, The New York Times, and the *New York World* newspapers were then published, to fulfill their Sunday obligation by stopping by on their way home after the Saturday night press runs. The "Printers' Mass" also drew many railway workers, postal employees, policemen, firefighters, brewery, and saloon workers.[2]

Peter started as an intern apprentice, learning furniture making and carving; he was a natural artist. He made $18 a month, less than at the tannery, but within six months, his talents were recognized as a first-class cabinetmaker, and his wages were raised to $30 a month, which was more than enough to upgrade their housing.

By the middle of the decade, more people began crowding into New York City, including thousands of newly arrived immigrants seeking a better life than the one they had left behind. In New York, the population doubled every decade. Buildings that had once been single-family dwellings were divided into multiple living spaces to accommodate the growing population. Most of the housing was cramped, poorly lit, and lacked indoor plumbing and proper ventilation.

The McNallys lived in those poor conditions for only a year, building up a nest egg so they could upgrade their living conditions, and they did.

After a year of living in the squalor of the Five Points slums, the saving and pooling of wages allowed the McNallys to move into the same neighborhood as the Cunninghams into a large apartment with two rooms on the second floor of a brick-tenement building. It even had a cast-iron stove for heat and cooking.

James and Peter were happy with the new home in a better neighborhood.

---

2 Wikipedia.

CHAPTER 10

New York City
A Growing Family
1859-1867

I t was 1859. The McNallys had been in New York for ten years. The years moved along and since their days in Dublin, and Peter McNally and Bridget Cunningham's friendship had grown. They still spent their Sunday afternoons walking and talking. Now it was more than just a friendship. They were falling in love.

One Sunday, they walked far north to where the dense city buildings and streets thinned out; there was a lot of open space, meadows, trees, and farming, reminiscent of parts of Ireland. It was a bright sunny day without a cloud in the sky. The northern meadow of farmland was void of people except for them. The farmers were all home, observing the Sunday day of rest.

Peter carried a sack with him, some bread and cheese, and a blanket. The willow trees in the meadow had just burst with new spring foliage, and one large one created an umbrella of drooping green branches. The couple had lunch under the tree on the blanket and talked about what the future might be for them.

"Peter, what would you like to do in the days to come?"

Peter looked at her, then turned away.

"What is it, Peter? Are you all right?"

Peter thought as he gazed into the distance through the hanging willow branches. He stared silently for a moment, then turned, looking straight into Bridget's brilliant blue eyes.

"Yes, I am fine, and here's what I want to do right now."

He put his right arm around her, leaned her back, and kissed her. It was a long, wet kiss and then another and another with happy moans. Bridget melted into his arms and responded with much enthusiasm. They made love for the first time. It was somewhat awkward, what with the removal of britches and moving bulky clothing aside, but it was a wonderfully happy event for both of them. There were moans and groans and, at times, giggles and laughs and even shouts. They continued until they were both limp, tangled up in the blanket, full of sweat, and panting with smiles and laughter.

On that day, Peter asked Bridget to marry him, and she said yes. Peter was twenty-six and Bridget, twenty-five.

The rest of the family was happy with the news, and the wedding happened a few weeks later at their church, St. Andrews.

In early December, only eight months later, Bridget gave birth to their first child, a girl. She was named Mary Agnes. The church ladies did the "from marriage to birth" math, and eyebrows were raised at the christening.

Right after their marriage, Peter and Bridget moved into an apartment right next to Bridget's parents. Sarah, now a grandmother, was always available to help Bridget with the grandchildren.

James also moved at that time into a small apartment in the same neighborhood.

By December 1859, Peter had been working for the furniture company for ten years. He really loved the work as it tapped his artistic talents; however, he developed severe arthritis in his hands, and he began making mistakes in his carving work, expensive mistakes.

The company liked Peter a lot but could not tolerate the costly errors, so right after the new year, Peter was given a lesser job, not involving his once talented skill. He was reduced to a common laborer with a cut in pay.

He was devastated and embarrassed to tell his family, so he asked if Patt could help him till he found a higher-paying job. Patt did just that and told Peter he knew a fellow at their church who worked for the *New York World* as a pressman and was told they were looking for workers willing to learn on the job. The good news was that the newspaper was Irish-friendly. It also was the leading voice of the national Democratic Party.

The next Sunday, Patt introduced Peter to Ian McGee, a pressman at the newspaper.

"Patt tells me that the *World* is hiring trainees; is that so?"

"Yes, it is," Ian replied. "And they will train you on the new presses, and in no time, you will be making what you were at the furniture factory as a craftsman. It's a union job."

Peter went to the newspaper, applied, and got the job. It was a bit dirty but paid well and didn't require fine motor skills. As an employee, the *World* gave everyone a free newspaper every day.

Ever since Peter got the job at the *New York World*, on most nights, when he was in a good mood, he would read the paper to the family after the dinner meal.

The whole family and most New Yorkers followed the national politics and the rumblings of a possible war in the newspapers.

In January 1860, Peter, James, and Patt all voted for Abraham Lincoln. That election served as the primary catalyst of the American Civil War.

Long before Lincoln's election, war drums had been beating in the South. William Barnwell Rhett penned the succession papers in his home on Craven Street in Beaufort, South Carolina, and in December 1860, South Carolina seceded from the Union. Within five weeks, they were joined by Mississippi, Florida, Alabama, and Georgia, forming a southern Confederacy. On April 12, 1861, the bombardment of the US garrison at Fort Sumter in Charleston Harbor took place. The country was at war.

Lincoln called for forty thousand volunteers to fight the South. The need for troops was almost immediately filled. Peter despised slavery and believed it was a practice spawned by the British culture and encouraged by them in colonial America. He always said it was such a "British" thing to do. He and his family always despised the British, saying, "When did they ever do anything good for the Irish, or for that matter, for America?"

He told James of his plans to enlist and asked him if he would care for his family while he went to war. He felt a responsibility to join the Union Army. James agreed, so Peter volunteered to fight, but he was assigned to a non-combative New York State engineering battalion. It was an inactive reserve unit throughout the war.

Late in 1860, Agnes was born, then in 1861, Catherine. For whatever reason, Peter did not feel close to Mary or Agnes. Actually, he was jealous because of all the affection Bridget poured out on them. He felt left out and ignored. However, when Catherine was born, he became very attached to her, perhaps because of her red hair and bright blue eyes. She reminded him of his mother when she was young. Peter affectionately called her Kate; she was to become his favorite daughter.

With the growing family, Peter rented a large apartment adjoining the Cunninghams.

In 1862, Edward was born; there were not many days when Bridget was not pregnant or nursing an infant.

For the next three years, life in New York City went on much the same each day for the McNally family. Peter had his job at the newspaper and was now making good money.

On April 14, 1865, President Lincoln was assassinated. The entire country mourned; at least the North did.

By 1866, James, Peter's half-brother, was getting sick of New York City. It was constant work, work, work with not much time for himself. He was tired of being looked down upon for being Irish and Catholic, and he decided most of the people in his neighborhood weren't worth getting to know. He was thirty-six and decided it was time to be on his own, but not in New York. He had been reading a lot about Philadelphia, the "City of Brotherly Love," and the opportunities there, especially for the Irish. So that October, James told Peter he was leaving for a new life in Philadelphia. He said he would leave them a good amount of money to help them get along and send more if he was successful in Philadelphia, and he knew he would be.

The family walked with James to the New Jersey ferry boat, which was scheduled to leave on the hour from the East River. James had contributed over the past six years to the family, but he also saved about one-half of his wages. He was excited about the opportunities he somehow just knew would be there for him.

Amid a few tears and hearty hugs, James boarded the ferry with his luggage.

James asked his stepbrother, "Now do ya have any advice for me?"

"I do, I do," said Peter. "Just don't make any mistakes."

They both laughed.

James stood on the stern, waving until the returning waves of good wishes disappeared in the distant midday fog.

Not long after James moved to Philadelphia, in the late fall of 1866, Peter and Bridget decided to take their children on an excursion. There was a ferry in the East River that crossed to Brooklyn and, on occasion, made a scheduled crossing to New Jersey. It was Monday, November 26. The ferry *Idaho* planned a crossing to Hoboken, New Jersey. It was a beautiful day with unusually mild temperatures. Peter was given the task of going to Hoboken to bring back new production plans for newspaper printing equipment.

This was to be a relaxed family outing combined with business.

The passengers filed off the ferry, and Peter bid his goodbyes to the family. Bridget, now eight months pregnant, waited at Hoboken ferry terminal with the children, looking back on the city and watching the passing ships and boats in the harbor. Peter took a carriage to his business meeting and was gone for about four hours. His return was timed to get on the return ferry at two o'clock.

While he was gone, Bridge went into early labor. She prayed, "Dear God, help me, help me." She remained still on the bench and occasionally moaned as the labor pains came closer.

The four children looked on and were not sure what was happening. Bridget told them, "The baby's coming. I'll be all right, I will." She tried to console them, especially Edward, who was only four.

Agnes, the oldest, had seen this before and said, "Mother, I will help you," and she held her mother's hand.

Bridget told them all to stay by her. As two o'clock approached, the pains were close and severe. When Peter returned, he saw the scene before him, and he knew before he reached her what was happening. Her water broke. Peter spread his coat on the ground for Bridget to lie on. A crowd had gathered, offering to help. One man said, "I'm a doctor. I can help you."

Peter stood up and stepped back. The children huddled around him as the doctor delivered the baby boy. Two hours later, they took the ferry back to New York. James was the only child to be born in New Jersey so far.

When the ferry docked at the East River pier, Peter summoned a carriage for Bridget and the baby. Peter and the rest of the children walked, leading the way back to their apartment. Bridget was nursing James as the family made their way home from the ferry when they heard a very large explosion that shook the ground.

On the last trip of the day, when the *Idaho* left the river pier and was in the middle of the East River, there was an enormous explosion and fire.

In a short time, it went to the bottom. Many people were pulled from the frigid water, but many perished. Peter read about it in the paper the next day where there was a drawing on the front page of the New York World showing people being rescued from the East River.

The family had been receiving regular letters from James in Philadelphia. He told them how he rented property in center city and opened a saloon, where he also had a room to live. He described how much less crowded Philadelphia was and that there were many Irish neighborhoods with good housing, not slums, and the rents were reasonable.

Bridget wrote return letters filling her half-brother, James, in on all the happenings in New York and about the growing family.

On hearing this, James urged the family to pick up once more and move to Philadelphia.

The McNallys finally got comfortable in New York, other than the crowded conditions. Renting a larger space was out of the question. The money was not there for that, and there were all those mouths to feed. This situation finally led Peter and Bridget to move to Philadelphia with their children. They were encouraged by James to make a move and that he would be there to help them get settled.

The McNallys met with the Cunninghams for the last time at church. In two days, they would be in a new year and a new city.

Bridget tried to urge her parents to join them in the move, but they said they were happy in New York and would remain there. They had too many friends at the church, and Patt was content with his job, making good money.

Bridget and her mother, Sarah, promised to write and stay in touch. It was just after the new year, 1867, when Peter, Bridget, the three girls, and two boys took the boat to the train to Camden. Not surprisingly, Bridget was pregnant again and due to give birth in a month. Before they left New York, Peter wrote to James, asking him to find a suitable place for them to live, and told him the most they could afford was $35.00 a month. James wrote back, saying he found a nice four-room place above a vacant commercial space in that price range, not far from center city, and would pay the landlord what was necessary to hold it for them.

Once their train tickets were secured, they wrote to James, advising him when they were scheduled to arrive. They had their things packed and were ready to start yet another new adventure in the "City of Brotherly Love."

By 1867, Philadelphia's foreign-born population, including many Irish, numbered over 170,000. Unprecedentedly, large numbers of the newcomers were Irish Catholics in a city that always had been a center of Protestantism.[3]

Philadelphia was about to have its population increase with seven Irish Catholics.

---

[3] Russell F. Wigley, et al (nineteen other author contributors), *Philadelphia: A Three-Hundred-Year History.*

CHAPTER 11

Jame's Move to Philadelphia
1866

I t was a year ago that James left the ferry and purchased a ticket to Camden from Hoboken, with a change of trains in Perth Amboy. He walked down the aisle, looking for a seat. The train was filled mainly with businessmen. He could tell by the more formal attire.

He said, "May I join you, sir?" and sat next to an older gentleman, who, like him, was friendly and gregarious.

The man introduced himself as Kenneth McPherson, a native of Philadelphia. He was a spirits merchant and was returning home after a few days of business in New York.

Kenny, as he asked to be called, took a keen interest in James. James told Kenny why he was going to Philadelphia, of his dissatisfaction with life in New York, and how he read of the job opportunities in Philadelphia. He told him how he learned the cooperage trade, one he was good at and learned in Ireland but was looking to find a job with less manual labor.

Kenny listened and said, "Young man, you seem like a very smart fellow. Would you like a bit of advice from someone who has been in business for some years?"

"Why, yes…yes, I would." James listened intently as Kenny spoke.

"Well, young man, you are on the right track. You are way too smart to be doing manual labor. My suggestion is, why make the barrels and kegs that hold spirits and beer? Why not sell the products to those who want them and make more money for yourself without the manual labor? You're not going to get any younger, you know. You can rent a place in the city center and open a saloon. Philadelphia is growing, and the people moving there, like you, enjoy their spirits and beer. You do now, don't you?" he said with a laugh.

"Yes, I do, Kenny. I've been known to have more than a wee dram or two at times."

They both laughed.

The conversation went on for the rest of the trip. As the train slowed and approached the Camden train-ferry terminal, Kenny said, "I tell you what, young man, I have a carriage meeting me at the dock and taking me to my home on Rittenhouse Square. Would you like to take the ride part way, anyway? I can point out the sights, and we will go by one area of the city center that has been crying for a new saloon. It's not much out of the way for me."

The carriage was sizable, and it easily accommodated both the men and their luggage. Kenny pointed out the cart vendors on East Market Street. They stretched from the waterfront on Front Street to well ahead of them, westward to Fifth Street.

The carriage turned south on Second Street. Both sides were lined with stately buildings and a lot of three and four-story brick residences, all with white marble steps and slate or cedar-shake roofs.

The streets were paved with granite "Belgium blocks," ballast from the ships left on the wharf and replaced by heavy cargo for the return trip.

They traveled south a few blocks, with Kenny giving a running narrative. They turned right on Walnut Street, went down to Sixth, then left.

James said, "You sure are taking me on the grand tour."

"Well, I am. I want to show you a building on South Street that would be perfect for a saloon. Actually, I have selfishly been trying to promote that use there so I could sell my products at that location. I know the owner and can introduce you."

They proceeded a few blocks, then turned onto South Street and up to Second.

One building from the corner on the left was a vacant glass-front building with a sign that read, "Lease or Buy. Inquire R. Whittier, 600 Chestnut St."

The coach stopped, and they both looked into the front window. It was perfect. The space went through to a narrow alley at the rear on Hudson Court.

"We'll go around, and I'll have the driver stop at the real estate office," Kenny said. He really took a liking to James and wanted to help him. While the coach waited, he made the introductions, and Robert Whittier walked James through the lease and sale agreement.

"Well, I'll be leaving now, James. Good luck. Take good care of this young man, Robert. And James, I'll stop by in a week to see how you are doing, okay? Take care now, and God bless."

James ended up with a minimum amount of down payment and a lease-purchase agreement for what would be his saloon. He would own the property in twenty years.

It turned out that James was a natural as a saloon owner. He decided to name his saloon, not after himself, but after the man who helped him. The sign across the front above the window and door read, "McPherson's Saloon." He copied the sign design from the O'Connor's Pub sign in the old New York neighborhood; it even had the two gold shamrocks at either end.

James didn't have an ego issue having to use his own name and, in many ways, thought it would be better not to, never knowing who your clients might be. *They were all drinkers*, he thought.

James hired a young man to help him finish the inside work. They were both good carpenters and built a bar, a small kitchen with a pantry, and a room in the back for James to sleep. In three weeks, the sign was hung, and he was open for business.

During this time, Kenny, the spirit salesman, stopped by and told him what he would need to stock the bar properly and gave him a payment plan; he also gave him a referral to a beer distributor, a friend of his. James kept in contact with Kenny, and Kenny continued to supply the saloon's spirits. His saloon was an instant success.

CHAPTER 12

The Final Pilgrimage—Philadelphia
1867

As with James's trip to Philadelphia the year before, the McNally family was fascinated by the train ride. This was something new for them. They sat in the last coach, right in front of the caboose, and watched the scenery speed by. They could not believe how fast they were traveling.

Kate sat next to her father. She was petite and cute, with long red hair and green eyes, looking much like her paternal grandmother.

"Father, what will Philadelphia be like?" she asked.

"Well, James told me it was very different from New York, not so crowded, and very friendly people. That's about all I know. We'll find out in a few hours, now, won't we?"

"I'm very excited," said Kate. "I think I will like it. I want to open a dress shop when I grow up if I can."

"And I'm sure you will," said Peter.

At the age of six, Kate watched her mother and Sarah Cunningham as they made dresses. From time to time, they would make time to teach her how to measure the pattern, how to cut the cloth, the right way to hold the needle, how to thread it, and the proper stitches for seams and hems. She was a good student.

"What will you do for work, Father?" asked Kate.

"Your uncle James told me there was a real need for grocery stores in many neighborhoods. I think that's a possibility. I don't know much about the grocery business, but it shouldn't be a hard thing to do. We'll see. I like the idea of having a grocery store, and besides, we will always have a lot of food available."

The train was chugging along, somewhere between Jamesburg and Cranberry. Bridget sat across the aisle from Peter and Kate. The baby was due in about five weeks, but apparently, the clacking rhythm and the side-by-side jostling of the train caused her to go into premature labor.

"Jesus, Mary, and Joseph!" she shouted when her water broke.

"What is it, Brige?" said Peter.

"The baby is coming," she said with some alarm in her voice.

This caused quite a commotion in the train car. The conductor came rushing back and put his coat on the floor. Peter reached up into the shelf above the seats and went into his luggage for a few blankets. He folded one for a pillow and handed the other to Agnes to hold up for a bit of privacy.

Peter told the conductor to run for some hot wet towels and some dry ones, too. By now, Peter was used to delivering his children when a midwife wasn't available; as with most of Bridget's births, the baby came quickly.

Peter announced it was a boy, to the cheers of the other passengers, just as the conductor returned from his mission.

The conductor said, "Well, sir, do you have a ticket for this lad?" There was laughter and more applause. They named him Joseph.

Bridget was nursing Joseph as the train pulled into the Camden terminal around noon. The day was bright and not too cold, and the sight of the Philadelphia skyline was something to behold, with the buildings reflecting in the Delaware River. The river was swarming with sailboats, steamboats, barges, and tugs of all sizes. As the ferry headed for the dock, it passed to the north of two islands close to the shore. Smith and Windmill Islands stood just off of the Market Street ferry terminal. They were separated by a narrow channel.

The McNallys all stood by the rail near the bow, taking in all the sights. They could see a lot of people on Smith Island, the larger one on their left, enjoying the fun of an amusement park, while in contrast, several mill buildings on the southern Windmill Island were obviously abandoned, as evidenced by their broken-down, smokeless stacks and lack of activity.

They were approaching the dock when Peter picked out James in the crowd onshore. He hollered, jumped up and down, and waved both hands overhead, shouting, "James!"

James heard him and returned an enthusiastic wave.

When Peter and Bridget saw James, they could not believe how much he had changed since he left a year ago. He was now thirty-seven and so handsome and grown-up-looking. He had wavy reddish hair and a short well-trimmed beard and mustache. He was dressed well, wearing heavy brown linen pants and a long brown coat. He was sporting a brown derby and, when greeting Bridget, who was holding the baby, he held his hat by the front brim and tipped it while nodding. It was a gentlemanly courtesy.

James said, "So what have we here?" looking at the newborn.

"His name is Joseph. He was just born on the train ride down here," said Peter.

"So good to see you all. It's been too long, but I'm glad you are all here now. You know it's only been a year, but my, how all my brothers and sisters have grown."

Bridget said, "Agnes is eight now, and Catherine just turned six, and, of course, the baby, Joseph. And there is Edward with your baby brother. He just turned four."

"My goodness, that's quite a beautiful and handsome family we have. I think you will all get to love Philadelphia. It is the City of Brotherly Love, you know. You know, when you own a saloon, you get to learn all sorts of interesting facts and lies, too," James said with a laugh.

"Let's go to the saloon now. I'll get two carriages and help mother and the baby into one. There's a lot of good food and drink waiting for you there, and your new landlord will be there to meet you."

They drove down Market Street. They had never seen so many wagon vendors in one spot. They lined both sides of the street for several blocks. Everything was for sale, from clothing, hats, shoes, vegetables, meat, seafood, milk, bread, and spices. The smell was a mixture of curry and the sweet odor of horse manure. Other than the droppings on the street, it was the cleanest street they had ever seen in a city.

They continued to Second Street and made a left turn south, where the houses and storefronts were mostly red brick with cedar-shingled roofs. All were raised from the street by two or three steps. In a few blocks, they turned right, just past Hudson Court, a narrow alleyway. The saloon was the second building on the left.

Peter noticed the privy just past the back door. Pointing to it, he said, "I'll be need'n that now. I'll be right with you in a minute."

The saloon was comfortably crowded, and James had reserved a table for himself and his family. He had hired a young man as a helper, who was tending bar and serving simple food offerings and soup. James introduced Liam to his family. "His name is Liam, but I call him Willy."

James went out of his way to provide a fine meal for his family. There was a butcher shop further down Second Street that cooked meats at lunchtime. He got an ample supply of cooked lamb and potatoes and some boiled beans he called "Lima's." He also had a dish of salt on the table. "I got used to putting this on my food. It's rather good. Try a bit." He had clear cold fresh water for Bridget and the children, while he and Peter enjoyed an ale.

James was quick to fix up the bed in the back room for Bridget and the baby. "Now get some rest until the food is ready."

"Oh, thank you, James," said Bridget. "You are one fine family man, you are."

The landlord was there and joined them around the table. He told them about the property he had for them at 510 Coates Street,[4] a few city blocks west and north from the saloon. He described the place as a three-story brick and wood building with two bedrooms on the second floor, plus an attic and basement; the first floor was large enough to be divided into rooms or used as a place for a business.

Peter asked the landlord what the rent was for the whole building as he was considering going into business.

---

[4] Coates Street was renamed Fairmount Avenue in 1873.

"That would be $35.50 a month."

"We'll have the money for that. We will rent it, and I'll open a grocery store there. Is that a good place for a grocery?"

"I think so. It's in a good residential area. There were no other grocery stores nearby. The property is not far from the train depot where the produce and meats come in from the farms in Lancaster County, west of the city. I can meet you there tomorrow, say late in the morning. I'm sure you will all need to be getting a long rest tonight after your busy travels. I will meet you there. Shall we say eleven o'clock, all right?"

"Yes, fine," said Peter. "I will meet you tomorrow at eleven."

The children played on the floor upstairs after the meal and fell asleep there.

"For the night, Bridget and the baby can sleep in the back room here in the saloon, and the rest can sleep here in the barroom after I close. I'll get you some extra blankets from what used to be my room in the back when I lived here. I rise early and will go across the street from my house to the bakery and bring us some fresh warm bread to have before you go to see the property. I think you will like it. Bridget and the children can stay here with me. I will enjoy being an uncle, but I guess I need some practice," he said with a laugh. James laughed a lot and was quite the charming young man.

In the morning, after they had their bread, James went to Second Street and gave Peter the directions.

James' directions were simple, as the street grid system of Philadelphia was easy to navigate, even for strangers.

As he got to Market Street, off to the right, street market vendors were setting up for the day. Peter looked to the West and saw a store at Eighth and Market and thought he would have a look.

Well, this won't be any competition to the McNally Grocery, he thought with confidence.

It was a medium-sized store. The sign read, "Strawbridge and Clothier—Dry Goods." They would very soon replace the small old building with one five-stories high and then expand into neighboring buildings as well, to the West on Market Street.

Peter arrived a few minutes after eleven. It was a fine-looking building, red brick with two large windows on each side of a wide door, which was open, with a wooden-sided second floor, with two windows and a cedar shingled roof with two windowed dormers in the attic roof. There was one chimney serving fireplaces on both floors, a door to the back at the bottom of the stairs, and a privy behind the building.

Peter thought to himself, *The good Lord has steered our path to this, our new home and store. Thanks be to him. Praise the Lord.*

It was the last day of 1867, the start of a new year and another start of a new life for the McNally family.

For the first couple of weeks, the family slept on the floor, a fine wooden floor, not a dirt one. The fireplace still had a small supply of wood they used to cook, and they had their daily meal right before it was time to sleep so that the cooking fire would take the chill out of the air. They slept with layers of clothing, coats, hats, shoes, or boots.

Peter bought some used lumber, a used saw, a hammer, and a bucket of nails; he bought some white paint and a brush. He fashioned a sign for the front of the building. It read, "McNally's Grocery." He thought to himself; *I'm in the grocery business now, I am,* looking at the sign and feeling rather proud of himself.

Each morning he would wake before dawn and wheel a hand cart along Coates Street to the railroad depot at Sixth Street. He met the northbound morning train from Lancaster County. He always enjoyed the early mornings ever since the days he worked on the farm with his father in Ireland. These mornings were especially enjoyable, watching the sky brighten. Upon reaching the depot, he would purchase fresh vegetables and other produce from the farmers, who rode the train along with their goods to the city. All the produce was fresh and in season; different meats, grains, flour, sugar, spices, milk, butter, and eggs were also for sale. The Amish stored the ice cut from ponds in many layers beneath the ground, separated by and topped with straw. It lasted into the summer and provided temporary refrigeration. It, too, was sold.

He would wheel the cart back to the store and set up a display in the cart on the sidewalk and put the other goods inside the store.

He then iced up the milk, butter, and other perishables and stored potatoes and other root vegetables in a shallow root cellar he dug out under the floorboards by the back wall.

As much as he wanted to be one, Peter was not a good businessman. He overlooked the fact that when he established his store, most of the people in what should have been his service area also bought directly from the train as he did at lower prices than what he charged at his store. Also, while there were no other grocery stores nearby, he overlooked the obvious. The Market Street vendors were just blocks away to the South. Some people shopped at his store for convenience, avoiding the walk to the depot or to Market Street, but many bypassed his store.

He kept poor records of his sales, often sold goods below what he paid for just to sell them, and often overbought perishable goods he could not sell, and when the ice melted, they ended up in the garbage. He was frustrated and beginning to feel depressed and very melancholy; the grocery business was not going well for Peter. While he had a great work ethic and put in the time, he was disorganized and couldn't figure out why things were going so poorly for him. *Why was this happening?* he thought. *I take my family to church every Sunday, and I feel like the Lord is punishing me.*

The family did go to church regularly at St. Augustine's Catholic Church on the corner of Fourth and New Streets. The church was built and dedicated only a few years before; somehow, it provided solace for Peter amid his continuing worries and woes.

As for Bridget, she and Peter spoke less and less. The church was her only refuge from Peter's increasing woes and foul moods. She often thought, *Dear God, all I do is pray to you, pray, pray, pray. Please hear my prayers.*

CHAPTER 13

Philadelphia
1867–1882
Births and Deaths

The days rolled by into the new year and then years into the next decade. Life for the McNally family was pretty much the same, day in and day out.

Peter struggled with making money at the grocery store, but at least customers were coming, mainly because Catherine was there helping and talking to them, while Peter remained in the background. Bridget and Sarah kept busy every day, taking the children to and from church school and working on their dressmaking and seamstress duties.

The family continued to grow. Sallie was born in 1870. As for Peter, what should have been a happy event was not. What should have been loving support for his wife and family was instead sullen moods and a failing business, which barely provided for the family's needs. With the lack of success, in spite of his long working hours and hard work, life was taking its toll on him, both physically and mentally.

Peter's distant former positive and persistent attitude was crushed. He was now more than melancholy. He was downright depressed; he was a broken man. He could not think straight. He became short in his words with Bridget in their daily conversations; he would become angry if she would even suggest anything she thought might help. "What the hell do you know about the grocery business, anyway?" he shouted back one night when they were in the store, taking inventory.

Bridget was astounded by his foul language, which made matters worse when she called him out. "That's not a proper language for a Catholic husband!" she shouted back. She was surprised by her loud and instant response. She had never reacted to him like that before.

The children upstairs in their rooms heard the ruckus. They became frightened and huddled in their beds. Peter, in silence, glared at Bridget. She had never before spoken like that to him. He turned and stomped out the back door, slamming it behind him, and disappeared into the night.

He walked east on Coates Street to the Delaware River and sat down on the rise, the top of the riverbank way above and overlooking the river and New Jersey beyond. The streets were empty. He was a solitary soul, and he felt just that, alone in the world.

What Peter did not know was that besides his business failing, the effects of working for the years in the tannery were manifesting their deleterious effects on his mind, an ugly combination of depression plus years of poisons ingested into his lungs, where it migrated to his bloodstream, into his brain, and into his bone marrow.

He didn't know it, much less understand it, but he was on a slow but steady downhill slide into the world of the insane.

It was one-thirty in the morning. As the full moon rose above the New Jersey horizon, it appeared larger and redder than a normal full moon. Peter stared at it.

What was that powerful force in the full moon? He didn't understand it, but he knew what it did to him. He knew it was real; it was trying to possess him. He thought it must be the devil in the moon, trying to seize, enter, and possess his mind and very soul.

Peter sensed this evil force, and he didn't like it; he forced himself to walk to the church, where he went inside to pray. He felt safe there, a place where the Devil could not get to him or possess him. He went to the altar, dropped to his knees, and prayed. After which, he fell to the floor exhausted, looking out one of the windows at the full moon.

"Ya can't get me in here. Ya can't. God, help me, help me."

Sleep finally swept over him.

As the sun rose, the beams of light hit a stained-glass window with the image of Jesus Christ carrying his cross. The refracted light beam painted a bright spectrum of light and color over Peter's face, causing him to wake up.

He did not remember the events of the night before, the many thoughts he had, or why he was where he was, nor did he question it. He just felt empty and confused. He recognized where he was and thought he had best go home.

When he got to the house and store, Bridget had just returned from taking the children to the church school, a block away from where Peter had just left. When Peter walked into their quarters above the store, Bridget said, "Peter, I was so frightened and worried, and the children were hysterical. Are you all right? I'm sorry we had words last night; I'm sorry. Are you feeling better? You know… about…the store."

Peter didn't remember all of what she was talking about. He just looked at her and spoke softly, "I'm all right." He was not.

As they ate the breakfast Bridget had prepared, she risked talking about Peter's worries; she knew if she didn't, another angry episode would eventually happen. She had to risk having the discussion.

"Peter, I know you have the worries about the store." As she paused, a flashback came to Peter. His mindset clicked, and anxiety filled him. Bridget could see it in his face. Before Peter could say a word, she said, "Peter, why not speak to James." She had never before given him any advice about anything and couldn't believe the words that just came from her mouth.

Peter just stared at her. She had never suggested anything that he should do. His mouth dropped open; he said, "Ahh…yes, James… yes, I will talk with James. I will go there now."

As Peter left, Bridget breathed a sigh of relief. With the stress of moving and Peter's wild mood swings, Bridget decided not to sleep with him anymore and didn't, regardless of her Catholic training to procreate the faith or the "duty," that she should accept her husband's often lust-filled advances. There would be no more babies. She would not do it. She was tired of being like a mistress for his pleasure and a "baby maker," at least for a few years. Actually, it would be two years.

James was a mature businessman, now forty; he learned a lot about how to run a successful business over the past years.

It was still early in the day when Peter walked into James' saloon. "Pete…well, how you do'n?"

"Well, James, I have the worries; I do."

"What's the trouble now, Pete? What are they?"

"It's me store. I'm not mak'n enough money; I'm not. It's a big worry, a real big worry, and I don't know what's wrong. Can ya help me now, can ya?"

"I'm not sure, Pete, but I'll try. I shouldn't think sell'n groceries should be much different from sell'n whiskey and beer. Take me to your store and show me how you do your business."

The brothers walked to the store, walked in, and looked around. Bridget was busy sweeping the floor.

"Well, James, it's good to have you visit."

"Pete told me of his worries, so I said I would have a look and see what the grocery business is all about. Pete, the store looks good, and I like your sign too. So tell me, how does your day start? Walk me through what you do each day. Maybe I can give you some ideas."

Peter told James he was up with the dawn and would take his wagon to the train depot to buy his meats and produce.

"Where's the depot?"

"Just down Coates Street. It's not far. The train comes in the morning and then again in the afternoon. One should be coming in about an hour."

"Let's go there. I'd like to see the depot and train."

They walked the few blocks west on Coates Street to the depot. On the way, James asked Peter if he had any competitive groceries near his store. He answered no.

"Where do your customers come from?"

"They're all around the neighborhood where the grocery is."

James was quietly thinking while looking at the scene before him.

Lots of people were gathered waiting for the train to come up from the center city, where it stopped first after coming in from the farms of Lancaster County.

Peter watched as his brother scanned the scene in silence as the train whistle sounded. The train had four boxcars, two loaded with fresh cut meats, mainly beef and lamb, but also boxes of sausages and tins of lard. The meats were quarters of lamb and beef and also smaller cuts in baskets. The other two cars had crates and smaller baskets of beets, turnips, leeks, cabbages, and onions.

At the loading dock, workers off-loaded the products onto carts that lined the dock. Peter pointed out that the larger quarters of meat were bought by butchers and the smaller cuts by local residents.

The same was true for the produce. Shop owners and owners of eateries would buy in bulk, and the locals would buy their weekly needs from the baskets on the dock. James saw wagons with store names on them loading barrels of rice, barley, oats, salt, and other barreled foodstuffs. None were available in small quantities, much like his saloon business.

"What do you usually buy for your store?"

"Pretty much of everything you see."

James watched the market scene intently. He was smart and intuitive, which is why his saloon business took off to instant success. He was told by Kenny, the whiskey salesman on the train, of the need to survey any area to see where the need was and who and where the competition was. Kenny did that for him.

He already knew his brother's grocery had no other nearby stores and that his customers were all around him.

As James continued watching the buying frenzy on the dock, he saw what was happening and did some thinking in his head.

As James was pondering, a young woman came off the dock with her basket of meat and produce. She headed their way and saw Peter. "How are ya, Mr. McNally?"

"Why I'm jus' fine, Kara. Meet me brother. This is James."

"And pleased to meet you, Mr. McNally. I must be getting along. I'll see you later at the grocery."

"Now, Pete, what does Kara buy at your grocery?"

"Well, let me think a bit. Usually barley, rice, bread, and other dry goods."

"Does she ever buy meat or produce?"

"Hmm…ahh, why no, I can't remember when she did."

James had Peter's situation pretty much figured out. It wasn't that his grocery wasn't in a market area. It was not that he didn't have a full line of meat and produce nor that he faced competition from other neighborhood groceries; Peter's competition was his own customers. It was just as easy for most of them, the younger ones, to walk to the depot and buy their produce and meat at nearly the same cost as what he paid for it in bulk.

"Let me ask you another question, Pete, 'Who are your best customers? Are they young like Kara, or are they older?'"

"Well, now…well, most are older. Yes, they are older. They like the store. They like me, and I get Kate to take their groceries home in a small wagon. They just love Kate."

"Why don't we start back to the store? We can talk along the way."

James explained to his brother exactly what he thought was going on. His younger customers had the energy to walk to and from the depot for their groceries, except for the things that Kara buys there that are not available other than in bulk on the train. He explained that the problem was that his store was too close to the depot, that it was not his lack of ability as a grocer to sell his goods, but the grocery was in the wrong location, and that his only good customers were older people.

"You need to move your store into an older neighborhood. You do, and when you do, you will do just fine. You will, for sure."

When they got back to the store, James explained to Bridget what was going on and said, "Don't blame Shawn, your landlord. He knows nothing about studying a market area and how your customers would do their shopping."

Peter said, "I feel like a bloody fool. I do. I should have looked around like you did for me today."

"Now, now, Pete, it's not the end of the world, you know. You can pick up from here and find a better place. You just have to go to other places and find out where the folks get their groceries and put your store where it is easier for them to get to. That's all you have to do. I can get Shawn to show you some other locations. He can take you there for a look-see, all right?"

Both Peter and Bridget felt better knowing what they had to do. Peter spent the rest of the week trying to sell off as much of his stock as possible. He also went to two other properties a bit further north and spent time there, looking around and talking to people who were carrying their grocery baskets and asking where they shopped.

He could see why what James told him to do was so necessary. Shawn, their landlord, found a larger apartment at 512 Coates Street to accommodate their growing family. Next to it at 500 was just the right size commercial space for the new McNally Grocery Store.

It was January 4, 1872. The McNallys moved to the new location, an older neighborhood, a good distance from the depot, with no other grocery stores in the area. Young Catherine, at eleven, loved to help her father in the store and talk to the customers, where her presence added so much to their shopping experience. Peter's new store became an instant success. His customers were happy to have such a nice store in their neighborhood, and there was no competition. The McNally bankroll steadily grew.

Peter's mood was lifted by the move; he had a new optimism and energy. In spite of Bridget's promise to herself, they went to bed for the first time in two years. After which, Bridget fixed some bread and cheese for them and hot tea.

She became pregnant with their next child, who was born in September of 1872, her fifth daughter, whom they named Angela, not after anyone they knew, trying to break what appeared to be an evil force from some demonic source cursing the family lineage.

Bridget was delighted with her new daughter. She would play with her and her two-year-old sister, Sallie, for hours on end. She loved making pretty dresses for them and showing them off to the ladies at church on Sundays.

Alas, the seeming bliss did not last for long. On April 30, 1874, Sallie died. She had contracted tuberculosis some months before. The entire family was devastated. The mourning never ended. The image of that beautiful child would never leave them. The funeral director recommended they purchase an entire "block" of grave plots, enough to accommodate the eventual demise of the entire family. The New Cathedral Cemetery at North Second Street and West Lucerne Avenue was several miles northeast of the family home.

Over the next two years, in the wake of Sallie's death, life again continued to be good for the McNallys, and once more, in November of 1876, Bridget gave birth again to her fourth son, Peter Joseph, named after his father and his father's favorite son. They all called him "PJ." PJ provided a special joy for both Peter and Bridget. He helped ease the loss of Sallie. They prayed that Sunday in church for the "Angel of Death" to stay away and spare their family from further harm.

The McNallys had been receiving regular letters from Mary, Peter's mother, back in Dublin. Mary told them how well the spirit business was going, so well that Daniel and Charles moved to Glasgow to open up their own business there. Charles had been in touch with a Scot by the name of Peter Dewars, who was experimenting with developing a blended whiskey at a more affordable price for the not-so-sophisticated pallet. He reported he was in need of some retail operators. Charles responded and advised him that he and his father were moving to Glasgow in a month to help Mr. Dewars with his needs.

As for Mary, the years in Dublin were very lonely. Daniel spent most of his time with Charles, and the marital relationship became virtually nonexistent. She wanted to go to Philadelphia and reunite with her real family.

At the time of this news, Peter and Bridget were in good stead. The store move was a good one, and one more person, especially Peter's mother, would not be a problem and would provide extra company for Bridget.

Mary had the money and traveled in style on a steamer from Dublin to Liverpool and then to Philadelphia; she arrived a month later.

The entire family met the incoming ship. If it were not for the fact that Mary said she would be wearing a bright red hat, they would have had trouble recognizing her. She looked so old, and so did they. Mary was ecstatic to be with her family and to meet her grandchildren.

Bridget received a disturbing letter from her mother, Sarah Cunningham. Her father, Patt, had died of smallpox; he was only sixty-six. "Peter, I know we are saving our funds, but we must go and be with her. She needs us."

Peter was in shock. Outside of his stepbrother James, Patt Cunningham was the best friend he ever had, one of the few that understood him and his moods, and now he was gone.

"Yes, we must go. I agree. I will see if the children can stay with James while we are gone. It won't be for long. Write a letter to your mother and tell her we'll be there as soon as possible."

A week later, Peter and Bridget were in New York. They knocked on the door of her mother's apartment on Worth Street. She opened the door, and seeing each other, they all broke down in tears.

Peter and Bridget tried to console Sarah. They stayed with her for the better part of a week. They went to church with her and reunited with the pastor. It was a good time spent by all. As their visit came to a close, Sarah decided she would terminate her lease and move to Philadelphia, as Peter and Bridget insisted. She would live with them. There was plenty of room, and she could have her own room and work with Bridget making clothing and doing seamstress work.

Peter decided to take a walk one night; he felt a need to be alone. His thoughts were about the premature deaths of both his daughter Sallie and his best friend, Patt; his emotions were a shambles. As he walked the streets of the neighborhood that night, there it was again, a larger than normal, blood-red, full moon rising over the Philadelphia skyline. He felt the feeling of impending doom once again.

Meanwhile, his business was prospering, his wife was happy, and all his children were doing well at the church school. Bridget was so pleased with Peter's newfound success and apparent happiness. They were happy together most of the time and quite amorous, so much so that Bridget became pregnant once again; and gave birth to another daughter. Bridget named her after her best friend, Genevieve. She was her tenth child and sixth daughter. The baby girl was so fair, so white, with a wisp of white angelic hair. They named her Genevieve which, in Irish, is *Gráinne* and means "white wave." She was such a sweet baby, so soft, so gentle, such a beautiful child.

Life could not have been better, or so it seemed.

A few months later, tragedy struck the McNally family again. In November, ironically, on Thanksgiving Day, five-year-old Angela died of smallpox. She contracted the pox three months before and was kept in quarantine, except for her older sister, who volunteered to be the family nurse and took the proper precautions to protect and disinfect herself. Alas, there was nothing she could do, nor anything the doctor could do to save her. There were no antibiotics available at that time.

During this time, almost one-third of all babies born died in their youth.

Angela was buried next to her sister in the Old Cathedral Cemetery.

In 1880, the city census listed the survivors of the prolific McNally family residing at 512 North 6th Street:

> Peter D, 47, Head of house, Grocer
> Bridget, 46, Spouse, Dressmaker
> Agnes, 20, Store Clerk
> Catherine, 19, Store Clerk
> Edward, 18, Store Clerk
> James, 15, Laborer
> Joseph, 13, Laborer
> Peter J., 4, Infant
> Genevieve, 2, Infant

Mary McNally, the first child, was conspicuously missing from the family census. Two years before, she could no longer put up with her father's shenanigans. Peter never liked her from the day she was born, and she grew up knowing that every day of her life and couldn't wait to make the split. She spoke with her mother many times about leaving, and at nineteen, the time was right. She moved to South

Philadelphia and never came back, although she regularly wrote to her mother.

Peter was his own worst enemy. His constant worrying about his business led to foul moods and depression, moods many of his customers didn't want as part of their shopping experience. They were happy to go the extra distance to the depot to avoid Peter. Peter saw his profits dwindle and blamed it not just on the store location. In his mind, his customers were the problem, not him.

The McNallys still lived at 512 North Sixth Street above the family grocery store. Peter was now forty-seven, and Bridget, forty-six.

Agnes, at twenty, was still living at home and helping her mother and Sarah with their clothing business. Agnes and Katie, still Peter's favorite child, helped their father run the store. Kate was good at dealing with customers and good at managing what to order and when. Agnes was good at managing the family's money.

The McNally boys, James, fifteen, and Joseph, thirteen, were on the Baldwin Locomotive Works payroll, working as common laborers, ten hours a day, six days a week. It was heavy, hot work, mainly moving heavy locomotive parts from the foundry area of the plant to the assembly area. They also did dirty cleanup work, but the pay was decent. The Baldwin Locomotive Works was one of the largest industries in the city. By 1882, the Baldwin plant covered more than eight acres and employed three thousand people. It produced over five hundred different sizes or styles of locomotives.[5]

The first two years of the new decade were relatively happy, prosperous ones for the McNallys, but then another tragedy was about to happen; it was forewarned by a familiar harbinger in the night sky.

On Monday night, August 28, 1882, a full moon rose over Philadelphia; it was a red moon. It was a supermoon, but it also was a "Devil Moon."

Peter hated the sight of a full moon. It always took him back to the time it tried to possess his soul, the night he spent in the church, and this night, it tried again.

---

[5] Wikipedia.

Peter felt an evil force within him and within his house. He woke everyone and lit three lanterns. He was sweating profusely.

"Father, what's the matter?" said Joseph in a concerned voice.

"I don't know, but something is wrong here. Something very bad is here, in this place, and I don't know what, but it's evil."

It was almost morning as the moon set in the west, just as the sun brightened the eastern sky and illuminated the McNally living quarters.

"Mama, I don't feel good," said Genevieve. Bridget went to her daughter's bedside. She had a harsh cough, and her face was red. Bridget put her cheek on Genevieve's forehead. She was burning with fever. Bridget had seen all her children sick from time to time, but she sensed this was something very serious.

"We must get Doctor O'Connor right away. Joseph, go for the doctor right now," said Bridget.

Doctor O'Connor's home and office were two blocks away on Fourth Street. He knew the McNallys very well and was a customer of the store. His wife bought dresses and other clothing from Bridget and Sarah.

Joseph ran the two blocks and pounded on the doctor's door. Momentarily, the doctor pulled the front window curtain to the side and looked out; on seeing Joseph standing there out of breath; he opened the door.

"Joseph, what is wrong with you?"

"I'm fine, sir. It's my little sister, Genevieve. She's very ill. Can you come quickly?"

"You go along. I'll get some clothes on and be right there."

The doctor examined Genevieve. "What's the matter now, little one? Are ya feeling poorly?"

She just wheezed.

"What is it, Tom?" Peter asked the doctor.

"I'm not sure, Pete, but keep her in bed, give her lots of water and hot broth, and have everyone stay away from her just in case she's contagious. When you go to her, wear a bandanna over your face just in case and wash your hands and face after each visit. I will come back tomorrow and see how she is doing. I'll give her half of this pill so she will rest better."

As the days passed, Genevieve's condition worsened. She developed a hacking cough, night sweats, and a bad headache. The doctor came every day, and by the end of the week, he diagnosed her illness as consumption or tuberculosis.

Genevieve started losing weight; three weeks later, she was dead. She was just four years old. The family was devastated by this, the third loss of a child.

Her small flower-covered coffin was set up in the front parlor, leaning into a corner of the room. Friends visited all day long and into the evening. The coffin was closed and covered in white and yellow roses. The next morning, it was carried from their house on a horse-drawn carriage to St. Augustine's for a funeral mass and then to the cemetery.

The family and friends followed in six more carriages. Genevieve joined her two sisters in the family burial plot.

When the family returned to their apartment, Peter gathered them together and announced, "We're leav'n this place, and I'm moving the store too. There's an evil force possessing this place. I'm sure of it, and we must get away from it."

CHAPTER 14

1882–1888
The Devil Follows

In the fall of 1882, the McNally family, minus Mary and Agnes, moved the store operations and residence further north to Eighth and Parish Streets. Agnes was the oldest child at home, and at twenty-one, she told her parents and the rest of the family that it was time for her to be on her own. She would not move with them but rather find a place in the neighborhood where she could stay close to her friends. If the truth be known, she had to get away from her father and his moods and eccentricities; she couldn't stand the constant stress. She saved some of the money from the monthly earnings that she gave to the family every month and had enough put away to start her own business. From her experience working in the family store, she knew the customers were always looking for fresh baked goods, which her father never had enough of. She had a good friend, an Irish baker. She would ask John Kelly to work for her and open a bakery shop. He agreed, and she did. It was very successful.

After a year in the bakery business, Agnes married John, and nine months later, she gave birth to a son. They named him James for her uncle James, whom she adored. The new son was the third James in the family.

Agnes kept in touch with the family, and from time to time, she would take a break from the bakery business to help out at the family grocery. She would often stay overnight with the family as her father was becoming more and more of a problem.

Sometimes, she and her husband would visit Uncle James at his saloon after shopping on Market Street. It was always a good visit for all. Young James liked to visit with Uncle James at the saloon and also visit with his grandmother Bridget and Aunt Kate, especially at their store. There was always something interesting going on there.

Peter tried to get his head together about his business problems, but for some reason, he couldn't shake the blue moods that surfaced practically every month, especially at times just near the full moon.

The grocery store on Parrish Street did not take off as it first did on Sixth Street, but why? What was he doing wrong now?

He checked the neighborhood, and there were no other grocery stores in the neighborhood, and it was an older neighborhood as well, which was supposed to favor his business, but he did not do a very good job in his surveillance.

Yes, the store was conveniently located, but from the day Peter opened, the neighborhood customers noticed Peter's foul moods. Ever since the death of his two young daughters, he never regained his once carefree, happy, and friendly personality.

While all the customers liked Kate, two months after the opening, she quit helping in the store and got a job of her own in a clothing store where she also took articles of clothing her mother and Sarah Cunningham made for sale at that store. Kate couldn't stand being with her father all day long. His craziness was rubbing off, and it was driving her crazy.

Peter was alone in his store, now a store in which customers no longer enjoyed shopping. If it were not for the money his sons brought in from the locomotive works and the money that Kate made from her part-time dressmaking, the family would have been broke. While they had accumulated savings, nothing was going to savings anymore. The store struggled for six more years with the few remaining regular customers.

In the summer of 1884, James, now eighteen, was still working at the locomotive works, but he wanted to get out on his own; he moved into a small apartment on Sixth Street; it was in the old neighborhood where he had lots of friends; they were a rowdy clan.

In September, he went to visit his family for the evening. When he arrived, he saw his father with a black eye and a missing front tooth.

"What the hell happened to you?" Joseph said with a puzzled look on his face.

"Ah, I got into a bit of a scuffle at the store today with that bloody Kraut, Koehnlein. He was giving me a lot of lip about how he doesn't like my store. Then the words started fly'n, and he called me a 'Schwein Hund,' so I punched his face, and he hit me back."

"Did you lay a good fist on him?"

"Only one good punch, but I fell down, and he ran out the door."

Two days later, on September 25, 1884, the following appeared in the *Philadelphia Times*:

> James McNally, age seventeen, who lives at 1744 North Third Street, was held on $800 bail by Magistrate Becker for committing an assault and battery on Andrew Koehnlein. Koehnlein is a baker and was out early in the morning to serve his customers when he was suddenly knocked down and beaten by McNally and Charles Collins of 1738 Bodine Street, who then took all the bread out of the basket and destroyed it, throwing the most in the gutter.

James and his friend were arrested and taken to Moyamensing Prison, the county jail in South Philadelphia, where they awaited trial.

They were both found guilty of assault and battery. Each was fined $500 and incarcerated for sixty days.

Peter, whom everyone now called PJ, the youngest son, completed his eight years in church school, and as with most families then, he needed to get a job to help support the family.

PJ saw an ad in the *Philadelphia Times*, "WANTED INTERN ENGRAVER, no experience necessary, will train on the job. Apply to Charles Elliot and Sons, Seventeenth and Lehigh."

When he read it, he rode the trolleys and walked some blocks to the corner of the plant and saw the sign over the door on Lehigh Avenue, "Charles Elliott and Son, Printing and Engraving." The building was a large red brick building taking up about half of the city block. He entered a small office area where several older men were doing paperwork, sorting through order forms and invoices.

"What can I do for you, young man?" the older man said.

"My name is Peter McNally. I saw your ad in *The Times*," he said as he held up the paper with the ad circled in pencil.

"So you think you want to be an engraver, do you?"

"Yes, sir, I would like that very much."

"My name is Charles Elliott. This is my company. Now can you tell me, do you have any artistic talent?"

"As a matter of fact, I do. I am a pretty good artist, at least, I think I am. It's my hobby."

"Well, young man, you are our first applicant. Could you come back tomorrow and bring some examples of your artwork for me to see?"

"Yes, sir. Yes, sir, I will. What time would be good for you?"

"Well, thanks for asking, very considerate. Let's say seven-thirty tomorrow morning. That's when I start work, and that's when you will if you get the job."

"I'll be here, Mr. Elliott. I'll be here. I really want the job."

When PJ left the Elliott plant, he was ecstatic. He liked Mr. Elliott and just knew he would like his drawings. When he got home, he told his father about his day. His father said, "What kind of job is that? Engraver? What is that anyway?"

"Father, it is part of the printing business. I don't know all about it yet, but they will teach me. Mr. Elliott wants to see my drawings. I'm taking them there tomorrow."

"Well, if it suits you, all right. Whatever you make will help the family."

The next day, PJ was up at sunrise; he took a box of his drawings, all pencil drawings, and sketches on heavy paper; there were street scenes of Philadelphia, portraits of people, and landscapes. He arrived at the plant entrance at seven o'clock.

Charles Elliott got off the early morning trolley right at the corner of Seventeenth and Lehigh. As he stepped off the trolley, he smiled when he saw his job applicant waiting at the door.

Elliott unlocked the door, opened it, and invited PJ in. He turned on a light and invited Peter to sit in a chair facing his desk.

"I see you brought your artwork."

"Yes, I did, sir. Would you like to see it?"

Peter took a pile of his drawings out and set them on the desk in front of Mr. Elliott.

Elliott looked at the one on top. It was a portrait of Kate that Peter did a few years ago.

"My, my, this is impressive." He continued to flip through and look at every piece. When he finished, he looked up at Peter and, handing him a piece of paper and a pencil; he said, "Write your name in your best script."

Peter took the pencil and wrote his name in a script that embellished the capital letters with a flair of whirls. He handed the paper to Mr. Elliott. Elliott looked at it, and with a smile, he said, "Young man, you just got yourself a job. Congratulations." He extended his hand.

"Thank you, thank you, Mr. Elliott. You will not regret hiring me. I will do a good job for you. I will."

"Don't you want to know what the wages will be?"

"Well, yes, sir, I suppose so. What are they?"

"You will start as an apprentice engraver. You will be paid 25 ¢ an hour for ten hours, six days a week. Work is from 7:30 to 5:30, Monday to Friday. Any questions?"

"No, sir, just thank you. When can I start?"

"Tomorrow."

"I will be here, and again, thank you, and by the way, they call me PJ." Then he laughed.

"All right, PJ, see you in the morning."

He left the plant and took the trolleys back home. When he arrived, he rushed into the store.

"Father, I got the job!" he shouted.

"What does it pay?"

"Fifteen dollars a week."

"Well, that's not that much, is it?"

"They will train me to be an engraver. The wages will get better as I learn; they will."

"At least you will be working and bringing in some money for the family."

PJ loved his job, and he liked both Mr. Elliott and the manager of the engraving department, a German, Everett Schmitz, who had been with the company for fifteen years and was an experienced engraver. He worked with Peter, teaching him the techniques of engraving on copper plates.

His department was responsible for creating the printing plates for invitations, announcements, and the like and adding names to trophies, commemorative plaques, and jewelry.

PJ's first project, all on his own, was engraving music notes onto metal printing plates that would be impressed onto paper that had preprinted staff lines on the final sheet music. He was a good student, and before long, he was promoted to master engraver and doubled his salary.

In 1888, the McNally family moved to a new residence and store at Eleventh and Master Streets. The move from Eleventh and Parish Streets to yet another location was what Peter considered a move from a cursed place.

In 1890, a city census listed the occupations and ages of the family members at 1403 North Eleventh Street, on the corner of Master Street. This was a recent move from what Peter considered a cursed location—their last home and store at Eighth and Parish Streets.

> Peter D, 57, Head of House, Grocer
> Bridget, 56, Spouse, Dressmaker
> Catherine, 29, Daughter, Clerk
> Edward, 28, Son, Clerk
> Joseph, 23, Son, Laborer
> Peter J., 14, Son, Engraver

By December of 1890, Peter finally figured out what was wrong, and it wasn't just his moods. Something was wrong with the business. He originally intended to see James again for advice, but he was feeling bad enough about himself. He had to figure this out by himself. He thought, *What would James do?*

Alas, Peter could not figure out what was wrong with his business or anything else in his troubled life; his mental state wavered more and more every day. He was downtrodden and a beaten man.

CHAPTER 15

1890-1893
Another Chance for Peter

As prosperity in the city continued, the High Street waterfront market expanded the only way it could, westward, into the center of Philadelphia. Accordingly and logically, the name High Street fell out of usage and became known as "Market Street," a better name for what it was.

By the time of the Civil War in the mid-nineteenth century, the various and sundry street markets, all open-air, now ranged six full blocks westward from the original Jersey Market at Front and Market Streets.[6]

For the past three years, along with his duties at the grocery, Edward McNally was on the advisory board for the new market being designed at Twelfth and Race Streets in the city center.

The market design filled an entire city block and enclosed 78,000 square feet of space divided into eight-hundred six-foot by six-foot stalls laid out in a grid system with wide aisles.[7]

The Reading Railroad tracks were raised, crossing Arch Street into the wide opening of a train shed on the second level of the building. At that time, the train shed was one of the largest single-span arched-roof structures in the world. Below the train shed was the market, and above it, five stories of office space.

---

[6] Wikipedia, Reading Terminal Market, History.
[7] Ibid.

The New Depot between Eleventh and Twelfth Streets replaced the previous open-air street markets in that block and on Market Street near Twelfth. The resistance and refusal of the market vendors to move to make way for the railroad depot gave rise to the ultimate design.

The head house, or part of the station that did not contain the tracks, was designed in 1891 by Francis H. Kimball, and the train shed by Wilson Brothers and Company. Construction began that same year, and the station opened on January 29, 1893.[8]

On February 22, 1893, Edward, his father, and his brothers attended the grand opening festivities scheduled as part of the city's bicentennial celebration. It all seemed like a good harbinger, one that the new year was starting off on a good foot.

Little did any of the McNallys know that later that year, this new grand marketplace would be the prime reason for their business to fail for the final time.

Peter's demeanor was getting worse by the day. Kate, who was the brains of the business, gathered the others together, along with her mother. Agnes took some time off from the bakery business to spend a few days with the family and to help Kate at the store.

Kate spoke to the group, "Father is getting worse. He is losing his mind. We can all see that. He is a total disruption to our operating efficiently and profitably. You can all see that too. Something needs to be done."

Agnes, now thirty-two and a year older than Kate, said, "Well, Kate, I think we all know that. But we just can't throw him out, can we?"

The others all nodded.

"That's not what I had in mind. I just want him out of here, and I think I have thought of a way to do it and actually make him feel good about it." They all looked on with interest. "Here's my idea. You know how the city is expanding not just south and west but north of us as well. Well, we are getting plenty of business here from the neighborhoods east and west of the store, so why not open a

---

8 Ibid.

branch store north or south of here and tell Father that we need him to run it, and we can take turns offering to help him."

Agnes spoke, "Kate, that is brilliant. I will be happy to look for locations starting tomorrow. I don't think we should tell Father until a lease is signed and we have the shelving, fixtures, and goods in place ready to operate."

Everyone agreed. In a matter of days, Agnes found the perfect property at Thirteenth and Girard, some blocks south of the main store.

Edward and PJ got right to work, building shelves, repainting the front door and trim, and even getting their father's original store sign, "McNally's Grocery," from the basement and installing it over the door.

"Father will be pleased to see this," said Edward.

Agnes, who was helping as the provisioner for the grocery, gave Edward and PJ a shopping list to drop off at the Reading Depot on their next trip to pick up provisions for the Master Street store. Two weeks later, the new branch store was ready to open, including an ad in the *Philadelphia Times*.

The family, without Peter, met again. "Who will tell Father?" asked PJ.

"Kate should," said Agnes. "She's his favorite, you know."

"Oh, lucky me," said Kate. "I don't know how much a favorite I am anymore, what with all his shenanigans around here, but anything to get him away from the store. Okay, I'll tell him tomorrow and try to be diplomatic about it."

Everyone was relieved that a plan was in place.

The next day, Peter was up to one of his occasional non-work activities. He was standing on the front steps, staring at the sky as if looking for something, and had Kate not interrupted him; he would have stood there most of the day. Going to the door, Kate said, "Father, can I talk to you for a minute?"

"Hmm, what?" he murmured as he turned.

"Father, we need your help. We really do," Kate began, trying to humor him and boost his ego. "Please come inside for a minute, would you?"

"Oh, ahh…yea…yes. How do you need my help?"

"Well, Father, you know how well we are doing here, thanks to you, so well that we need to open a branch store a bit further south to serve that expanding neighborhood. We all met and agreed you would be the best one of us to manage it. You know the grocery business so well."

Peter smiled for the first time in years. "Yes, I would be, wouldn't I? I would be the best one to manage it."

Kate knew how to stroke his ego, and it worked. She continued to pour it on.

"Oh, Father, we all knew you would say yes. Thank you, thank you. Agnes found the perfect store, and the boys stocked it for you. Would you like to see it? It's ready to open, and it will be your store. It's at thirteenth and Girard, a nice corner location, and it has a two-room apartment above it, and Father; I would like to move there with you to help you with your meals and housekeeping. The store will be yours to run. Your mother will be moving there too. She wants to be with you. She's been lonely."

"Oh, yes, I would like to see it, and thank you, Kate. I know we have not been on the best of terms lately, so maybe this will help us both, and I would welcome my mother to be there too."

"Edward will be back soon from running an errand. He will take you there, and if you need any help, just let me know, and Agnes can place the restocking orders for you, and Edward will bring them to your store."

Agnes made sure Peter's branch store had a residence upstairs so he would be away from both home and the main store most of the time. She would fill in for Kate when she was with their father, although Kate would still be in charge of running the main store. She would be with their father in the morning and evenings and keep an eye on him.

Edward took Peter to the branch store the next day. When Peter saw his old sign, he smiled broadly. "Yes, it's my store, isn't it? There's the sign I made."

"Yes, Father, it's all yours."

They went in and saw all the well-stocked shelves and then visited the upstairs residence, complete with a made-up bed and most of Peter's possessions and clothes, washed and hung up or folded and put in the dresser. There was a separate bedroom and sitting area for his mother. There was no reason for him to return.

"Father, I will bring the rest of your things here this afternoon. You can open the doors for business tomorrow. Congratulations."

With all his depression, his emotions could be like a roller coaster and could bounce back in a moment if something good happened, and he viewed his move to the branch store as good. *My children do trust me. They do*, he thought. *And Katie, my Katie, does love me.*

This arrangement worked for the better part of two years. By this time, the rest of the family felt any of Peter's problems were far away from involving them.

CHAPTER 16

1893
Another Bad Year

The winter of 1893 in Philadelphia was one of the worst on record. Snowfalls averaged five inches almost every week in February, with temperatures near or below zero. The Delaware River was frozen, shore to shore. People walked on the ice or took horse-drawn sleds to go back and forth to New Jersey. Overall, many businesses were paralyzed by the ice and snow.

During this time, Agnes again left her husband to do all the work at their bakery business so she could help at the family store. Ironically, the McNally stores did better than average for winter sales, both the main store on Master Street and Peter's smaller branch store, as the trolley service to Reading Terminal Market was out of service due to the buildup of ice over the streets and trolley tracks.

But with the spring thaw and all the publicity in the newspapers, customers in the area around the stores started to flock to the newly opened Reading Terminal Market. It was large, enclosed, and a novelty for all Philadelphians. Everyone wanted to see it and experience shopping there, and when they did, they wanted to return. While it was indoors and out of the weather, many people couldn't get to it because the trolley system was out of service due to the ice and snow.

When spring came, and as the ice and snow melted, so did the McNally businesses, but mainly Peter's branch store. Peter's initial positive spirit was just that, a spirit not lasting very long. Mentally, he sunk lower than ever. This periodic up-and-down syndrome seemed to follow him most of his life and wasn't stopping now.

Once again, location and demographics came into play as a primary cause of the business woes, but so did the attitude and eccentricities of the failing owner.

The primary store had an ideal location, at the corner of Eleventh and Master, in the heart of a mature and older client-based neighborhood. The customers were loyal. They were used to shopping there, and they had a good relationship with Kate, the store manager, and Agnes as well. The customers were older, and they didn't want the hassle of taking a long, round-trip, trolley ride to the Terminal Market.

Peter's branch store, on the other hand, was much further south, in a new yet expanding neighborhood. The customers were younger families just moving in. The store was close by, but they had no loyalty to shop there, and certainly not to the often grouchy, unfriendly owner, plus the idea of taking a long round trip trolley ride didn't faze them a bit. It was kind of an adventure, and the Reading Terminal Market was an exciting, vibrant place to shop, out of the weather, with crowds of like-minded young people, and all sorts of meats, fish, produce, and delectable delicacies and treats, in addition, sit-down breakfasts and lunches were served. These were not available at either McNally store. It was no contest, not even close.

So the stage was set for yet another failure for Peter to face, a failure at yet another time and yet another location.

Peter was his own worst enemy. The worse his business became, the more miserable and depressed he became, driving off the last of his customers.

During the brutal winter of that year, his customers would trek to the main store on Master Street rather than be subject to his aberrations.

Peter threw in the towel and admitted defeat to himself, which was self-evident. He could not deny it. His business was dead, and it almost killed him. At one point, he thought of taking his own life, but in his formidable style, it was easier to blame others. Someone had to be blamed.

He didn't take it well. He went back to the main store and spoke to Kate. "Kate, it's just not working down there. They are different people who live there. They are. They seem not to like me for some reason. I'm going to have to move the goods back here and close down."

Kate was no fool. She knew if she ran that store, she could make it succeed but in no way was she going to suggest trading places with her father. She also knew the main reason for opening that branch was to get him out of the main store's business. He was like poison.

Kate tried to humor him by saying, "Father, it's not your fault now. It's a different neighborhood. It's not that they don't like you. It's just that nobody knows you. Let me talk things over with Agnes and Edward, and we'll work things out. We will."

She could see he was upset and anxious, not knowing his fate, so she tried to humor him some more. "Father, it will work out all right, believe me, so for now, go back to your apartment, get some rest, and tomorrow morning, I will send the brothers up with the wagon to bring the remainder of your goods here. Just get a good rest, and I'll come by for breakfast tomorrow, okay?"

Kate thought she handled that very well, as she knew he could fly off the handle when troubles with uncertain answers surrounded him.

That evening, when the store was closing, Kate spoke with Agnes and Edward, telling them of their father's visit that afternoon.

They, like Kate, were initially uncertain of what to do, but one thing they all knew, he could not be involved in running the family store. "What can we do with him?" said Agnes. "This is a major problem."

"Look," said Edward, "Father is almost sixty-two. He should be retiring. You're right. We can't have him around here, sticking his nose into everything and annoying the customers, so we need to think of something to keep him out of the store. We don't need any money from the branch store. We never did. So what can we do?"

Kate, as always, was listening and thinking at the same time. "You both know Father, he can't take any criticism, and he loves praise. We have to use praise to get our way. He's coming for breakfast. Leave the discussion to me. I got him out of here a year ago, and I can again. I'll tell you what I have in mind. I will tell him we all met, and we all knew what a great job he did starting this store and the branch store. That the branch store was in a bad neighborhood, and that was not his fault. We should have recognized that. It was our fault. I'll tell him that for all his work, he deserves to retire and have us support him because he supported us for so many years."

"That's good," said Agnes. "But where will he stay?"

"Well, we have to rework the lease where he is so we can get the store off the lease and keep the rooms above where he can live. We don't have room for him here, and he knows it. And his mother, at almost eighty, needs to go into a home where she can get the proper care. We can't take care of her here. She should go into the Little Sister's Home."

Since Kate took the lead, Agnes and Edward just agreed. Neither of them was that gratuitous to try to solve this current situation with their father or his mother.

Kate thought the only way to keep her father physically out was to move herself in with him. She knew she could tolerate that, at least for a while, until a better plan could be devised. So the next morning, Kate took some eggs, sausage, and bread and went to talk with her father. She made breakfast and, while they were having tea, she tried to reveal her plan gently.

"Father, as I told you last night, you need a rest. The stress of running the store is not good for you, and I want to help you. Would it be all right with you if I moved into the room next to your room that you are now using to store goods for the store? I would like to help take care of you. I will cook the meals and bring you lunch every day and, in between, you can visit some of your friends in the neighborhood. You deserve to be able to do that. You have worked hard all your life providing for us. You need to stay away from the store and trust us to run it for you. You do trust us, don't you, Father? You taught us all we know," she lied.

Peter thought and said, "But what about my mother? Where can she stay?"

"We thought about that, and we think she would get the best care at the Little Sister's home."

Peter had no alternative but to agree. After a long silence and several sips of tea, he said, "Well, well, yes, I suppose that would be good. Thank you, Kate."

Kate had to hide her joy and instead just gave her father a kiss on the cheek.

"So then, I shall have the boys come here with my things and clean the place up a bit. Father, you will like your retirement. You can spend time with your friend Kro, you know, Kroberger, the German, go and visit. I'm sure he will be glad to see you, and you can probably give him some good ideas for his store. He's really not a competition, you know."

This arrangement worked very well for about four months when Kate was starting to feel the stress of her daily exposure to her father. Another family meeting was held, and Kate announced she needed a substitute. "I need a break from this. Someone else has to volunteer to live with him for a while," she said as she looked straight into Joseph's eyes.

"All right, I'll do it, but how do we explain the change in roommates?"

Kate answered, "I'll talk to him tomorrow and tell him. I really need more time at the store, and besides, you keep talking about how much you miss him." They all laughed.

"All right, I'll be the next victim," Joseph said while shaking his head in disbelief. "How did this happen?" he said.

"You're just lucky, I guess," said Agnes.

CHAPTER 17

The Estrangement
September 1893

Joseph's living with Peter lasted for only three months when he announced his marriage to Nora, a local church woman he had been courting since the beginning of the year. He had saved a good portion of his wages from the locomotive works and some of his share of the profit from the McNally grocery store. He and Nora planned to move to the Grays Ferry area of South Philadelphia, where Nora's parents lived. Joseph wanted his own life free from the day-to-day drama with his family.

So at the family meeting, it was decided to end the lease of Peter's residence and move him into Joseph's old room above the store.

Peter was happy to be back with his family, but seeing the store, he realized it was his no more. Agnes, who at first wanted to commit her father to an institution rather than have him move back, insisted that if he were to move back in, he would have to sign over the full and rightful ownership of McNally and Sons Grocery to her, the oldest child; she planned to partner the store with Kate.

Kate did not tell her father about the commitment order Agnes wanted to move ahead with but told him another lie, that a new law was in effect that required the owner of a business to be actively involved in the business. "Father, you must sign this for the good of the family. Agnes and I will be running the store. You need a rest." He signed it.

Peter's mood that week was not good. He was bored, although his children had tried to restore his self-worth by suggesting retirement was best for him. He was once again wallowing in the familiar depths of despair.

He was deeply depressed because of the failure of the branch store, one of now a series of failures. He couldn't shake this one, and while he blamed others, deep down, he knew it was his failure.

All that week, he would sleep late, wander down the stairs, through the store, and out into the street.

After standing on the street corner for several hours, he would go to the saloon, have some lunch, and sit and drink the rest of the day away. Peter had never been much of a drinker, but he was trying to soothe his depression and drown his sorrows. He started drinking at lunchtime and into the afternoon. For a few days, he always managed to come home at dinner time, but the dinners were silent.

There was not so much as a grunt from him or any of the family, including Bridget, who was afraid he would become violent if anything were said.

In the mornings, Peter would wake up in the small bedroom above the store. By now, he had accepted that he would never sleep in the same room, much less the same bed, as his wife.

He generally slept later than the rest of the family. Kate would open the store at eight o'clock, while Bridget would remain in her bedroom until the girls let her know Peter was up and had left the building.

When Peter came down the stairs and walked through the store, his daughters would keep their eyes on their work, not acknowledging his presence.

Fortunately, Bridget's mother, Sarah Cunningham, did not witness all this daily drama involving Peter and the family. She was very old and not that well, so she was placed in a home for poor and elderly women that was run by the Little Sisters of the Poor, which was founded by St. Malachy's church. Members of the family would often visit, as it was just a few blocks north on Fifteenth Street. None ever told her of Peter's condition and situation. Mary liked her new home and the many friends she had there from church.

Bridget could not concentrate on her usual housework, dressmaking, or the family business. Her mind was constantly spinning in fear of her husband; she did not know what to do except fear the worst, and she didn't know what that might be.

One particular evening, when Bridget retired to her bed, her fear and worry started changing to anger. She was furious. She tossed and turned in bed. Sleep was not meant to be.

Peter had left the store early that afternoon. He stood on the street corner for hours, as he had been doing all week, just looking up to the sky, then crossed the street, went into the saloon, and didn't come back for dinner at the usual time. This particular night, he was not back at the family's usual bedtime; he came staggering back into the store in the middle of the night.

Bridget was still awake and could hear him coming through the store, bumping into things that fell to the floor with a crash. With all the clamor, Agnes, who was staying for the night, Kate, Edward, and PJ were aroused from their sleep. They came into the hallway and looked toward the top of the stairs.

PJ, seventeen, was in a room at the end of the hallway. He stood behind Agnes, thirty-two, the oldest daughter. Both were trembling in fear. Bridget had left her bed and was already at her doorway with her hands braced on either side of the doorway as Peter crawled onto the hallway landing. Bridget was seething. She looked at this pathetic scene with Peter, drunk and still kneeling on the floor.

The hallway was dimly lit, with a small oil lamp on the wall near the top of the stairs. His children all saw their father crawling up over the last steps onto the landing, where he remained on his hands and knees. Kate called out, "Father, are you all right?"

Peter looked toward Kate and Bridget. He just stared, saying nothing. His head was slightly raised, his mouth somewhat opened, with saliva dripping down his bearded face.

Bridget, all of a sudden, snapped as though something else was controlling her and her words. She shouted loudly, "You get your drunken self out of this house, do you hear me? I'll have it no more of this or you! Get out of here now." She screamed, "Boys, get your father's clothes and things together! Put them in the small trunk, the one with the old blankets in it. Throw his clothes right on top and out the door with it, and with him too. Do it now!"

"But, Mother—" Edward, the older son, said.

"Edward, do as I say. I am in charge of this house now, and PJ, you are to help your brother."

Peter was too drunk even to try to argue. Bridget's loud, seething anger took him by surprise.

"And take all his keys away from him. He'll have no use for them anymore."

Her children looked in shock. They had never seen their mother act this way, yet she was so much in charge. "Do it now...I said, now!"

Edward and PJ helped their father down the stairs, as he could hardly walk on his own. Katie was hysterically sobbing, and Agnes said, "Mama, you can't just throw him out like this. Maybe we can get him committed."

"I can throw him out, and I just did. I will have no more of him in my life or in yours. He is a madman, and we can no longer have him in our family. He's a danger."

And with that, Bridget ordered the rest of the family to go back to bed, "Say your prayers for your father, for all the good it might do."

The brothers practically dragged their father, now almost unconscious, from the day-long drinking, down the stairs, through the store, and out to the street.

Edward said, "Let's take him across the street to the saloon. It's closed now, but one of his friends will help him in the morning when he wakes up. PJ, drag his trunk and follow me."

A light rain had started, and the sky was black with just a few wisps of moonlight as the broken clouds moved slowly across the sky. Other than brief glimpses of moonlight, the only other light was from a few dim gas streetlamps that made large glowing yellow circles about them in the foggy air.

When they reached the saloon, they pulled the trunk up the few steps to the door under the cover of an overhang. They pulled a blanket from the trunk and, after taking their father's key chain from his belt, propped him up against the trunk and covered him with the blanket. Edward, the oldest of the two, told PJ, "Go back to Mother now. I will be along in a minute."

Edward reached into his pocket and found a roll of bills, yesterday's receipts from the store. He was supposed to take the money to the bank that morning, but it didn't happen. He took almost half of the money, folded it, and placed it in his father's coat pocket. He then returned to his home across the street.

He securely locked and barred all the doors. He closed and locked the window shutters and went upstairs, which now was quiet. Everyone had returned to bed.

The sun was just starting to brighten the early Sunday morning sky when Patrick, the local precinct officer, was making his rounds down Master Street. He spotted Peter still asleep and slumped over. He rapped Peter's foot with his nightstick. "Pete, what the hell are you doing out here? Are you all right?"

Peter slowly opened his eyes. His vision was blurred, and his mind was confused. Slowly, he remembered the events of the night before. Bridget's words were still screaming in his head.

"She threw me out. She did. That's what she did. They all threw me out. They did. I can tell you, Patty, she won't be see'n any more of me; none of them will. I don't need them. I never did, and after all, I did for them. I raised nine children. I did. And they were good ones till she turned them on me. She turned them. She did, my own children. Well, I don't need them anymore either."

"What will you do, Pete?"

"I can take care of meself. I can. I don't need those grocery store problems anymore or the lot of them. I can take care of meself."

"Let me help you up," said Patrick. "Where will you go?"

"My brother James has a small room behind his saloon. It's not far from McGillin's Ale House."

"Can ya make it there with that trunk an all? I'd like to help ya more, but I got my rounds ta do, ya know."

With that, Peter put his hand into his coat pocket, feeling the bankroll. When he pulled it out to have a look, his eyes bulged wide open at the sight.

"Ya see, Patrick, me boy, I don't need that family no more... no more. I can take care of meself. If you would just help me to the corner and I'll get the early trolley, I'll be just fine. I will. I can find some help when I get to the city center."

The two men dragged the trunk a block to Tenth Street, where the clip-clop of the trolley horse echoed on the otherwise vacant street and then broke into view through the shroud of morning fog.

Several hours later, Bridget and the family got dressed as usual and attended Sunday Mass as though nothing had happened the night before.

As they left the store for church, James looked across the street to where they had left their father and hoped someone had helped him, as he and his trunk were gone.

CHAPTER 18

Devil Moon over Philadelphia
1893

On September 25, 1893, Peter McNally got off the southbound Tenth Street trolley at South Street. He gave the driver a few coins and asked him to help get his trunk from the second car to the sidewalk. He made his way to his stepbrother's saloon, dragging his trunk with leather straps that contained his small amount of possessions. It was almost noontime by the time he got to the saloon. It was busy with customers. He dragged his trunk inside and found James working behind the bar.

"James, I need your help," Peter said.

James came from behind the bar and looked at this brother. "What in the name of the saints happened to you, Pete? You look a mess," he said.

"James, I need a place to stay," said Peter.

James asked a few of his regular customers to take his brother's trunk to the back room. "Find a seat, Pete, and I will get you some soup and bread. We'll talk later."

That night, when the saloon closed, Peter told James how his wife turned his own children against him and took his business away from him. James had known over the years how his brother was declining mentally, so he just listened and offered to help him. "I can use some help here, Pete, cleaning up, running errands for food and supplies. You can stay here and be fed as well."

Peter lived with his stepbrother James in a small room at the back of James's saloon for about a month.

James was well aware of Peter's mental issues. He humored him and did not confront him. He would do almost anything to help him.

One night, after the saloon closed, Peter decided to go out for a short walk and get some fresh air after the events of the day. As he walked east on South Street, he stopped for a moment to catch his breath. He sat on the steps of a grocery store not far from the saloon. He looked at the sign on the window, "Duncan and Sons Grocery."

He thought of the store he started five years ago, his store, the very business he was thrown out of last month. He felt both melancholy and angry. He looked around. The street was empty of people. It was almost eleven.

He looked to the east. The night sky was getting brighter by the minute. As he continued to watch the sky, a full moon broke the eastern horizon, a full moon, a moon he remembered seeing before. It filled him with fear. It was a deep red-orange moon, almost blood-red. It captivated him in such a way that he could feel his melancholy being taken over by some inner, strange, and powerful force over which he had no control.

He continued to sit and stare at the full moon, mesmerized, for almost an hour, practically hypnotized, before returning to his room at the saloon. Although Peter felt what he felt, he did not realize it was a Devil Moon he was looking at, a Devil Moon rising over Philadelphia.

On Saturday, October 14, 1893, at 6:00 a.m., Peter McNally was restless. He didn't sleep well that night. He tossed and turned in his bed, his mind telling him he must move home. It was his home, his store. He finally drifted into a deep sleep, and when he awoke, it was morning. He had a plan.

He was going to move back in with his family and resume running the grocery store at Eleventh and Master Streets. He was fearful of both the trip back to the store and fearful of confronting his wife and children, but he had to do this.

He opened the back door to pee in the alley. He didn't bother with the privy. The alley was brightly lit by the full moon. As he turned to the left, he saw the moon once again, just beginning to set in the west over the Philadelphia skyline.

Peter was a nervous wreck, paranoid, and seemingly possessed. He was packing his small trunk, preparing to go home. Just getting to the trolley worried him. He was sure he might be attacked and robbed. He looked into the bottom of his trunk under the blankets that were there when he left the store. He found an old Colt revolver he bought when they first moved to Philadelphia, thinking he might need it. And there, in the corner of the trunk was a pasteboard box of 0.38 caliber bullets; he loaded the gun and stuffed it in under his belt on his left side and pulled his jacket over it. He felt safe now for the trip back home.

James, in the next room, heard his brother mumbling something and said, "Pete, you all right?"

"Of course I am!" Peter shouted back.

"Anything the matter, Pete?"

"Nothing is wrong. Everything is just right. I am going home," he said.

"You're going home? Do they know you are coming?"

"They will soon enough. They will when I get there."

"Well, do as you must. I have to meet some friends in a little while. Can I help you with your trunk to the trolley?"

"Thanks, yes," Peter replied.

"Do you have any of the money left that I gave you last week?" asked James.

"I do, enough to get home."

James attached leather straps to the steamer trunk, and the two men dragged it along the stone sidewalk seven blocks to the Ninth Street trolley.

"I'll wait with you till the next trolley comes and help ya with the trunk," James said. "I see one just now down there. It will be here in a few minutes."

After helping his brother with the trunk, James said, "Goodbye, Pete, and good luck. I'll be hopin' things work out for ya. I'll come up to see you sometime soon. I will."

Peter got on the trolley and paid his fare to Master Street.

After lots of stops, the trolley finally got to Master Street. Peter gave the trolley driver a few coins to help him get his trunk onto the street. The trolley stop was only one block east of the family store. He grabbed the straps and pulled them along behind him.

Peter had not seen the store or been in the neighborhood for nearly a month. He looked at the green awning, wrapping the corner sidewalk with "McNally and Sons Grocery." Its color had faded over the years, but he remembered the day he and his boys put it up. *It's my store; nobody else's,* he thought.

James Kelly, Agnes McNally Kelly's nine-year-old son, was minding the goods outside the store. James saw his grandfather approaching and ran into the store where Peter's daughter Kate, thirty-two, was behind the counter, shucking oysters for the corner saloon across Master Street. James rushed into the store. "Aunt Katie, Grandfather is coming with a trunk!"

Kate looked stunned but returned to her work and said, "James, return to your watch outside."

The sound of the trunk bumping up the steps into the store caused Kate to look up from her work. "Father, what are you doing here?"

"I'm moving back into my house and my store. Call the boys to carry my trunk upstairs."

Peter stared at Katie. "Father, the boys are not here, and you are not welcome here; you know that. You must leave here now. You signed the store over to Agnes when you left. Surely, you remember that. It was only a few weeks ago we reminded you of that."

Peter had no such recollection. Peter's stare became more intense as he slowly moved toward the counter. His complexion turned red, and saliva was dripping from his mouth over his lips and onto his beard. His mouth was slightly open, and his teeth were grinding. He was making a primal, guttural sound, almost a growl. He reached across under his jacket with his right hand and found the revolver he put under his belt on his left hip. He pulled it out and lunged toward the counter, holding the gun in two outstretched hands. He pointed the pistol at Kate's left breast and pulled the trigger.

The muzzle of the gun was almost touching her when the shot was fired. The sound echoed up to the living quarters where Bridget was doing housework.

Peter then leaned over the counter, bent over it, and, standing on one foot, fired another shot down at Kate, lying on the floor; it went wide of its mark. The recoil from the shot sent Peter, now off-balance, to the floor, still holding the smoking gun.

Bridget, on hearing the shots, screamed and rushed down the stairs. James ran from the doorway and hid behind some boxes on the sidewalk.

The noise from the shots must have jarred Peter's brain and thoughts. For now, he was back into reality, but not really sure of what just happened, but realizing where he was. He got to his feet, still holding the revolver. Seeing it, he tossed it into an empty bin, covered it with some paper bags, and left the store. He walked calmly across Master Street and entered the saloon, where he bought a newspaper, folded it, and put it in his back pocket. He continued walking up Master Street.

By this time, Bridget was in the store screaming hysterically for help and tending to Kate, who was bleeding profusely on the floor. After James saw his grandfather cross the street, he went back into the store.

"James, go find a policeman and have them send an ambulance coach!" Bridget shouted.

The police arrived and sent for an ambulance coach, which took Kate to St. Joseph Hospital on Girard Avenue, a ten-minute horse-drawn ambulance ride away.

She was still alive and conscious. The policeman in the ambulance asked, "Who shot you?"

"My father did," she answered.

When Kate arrived at the hospital, she was in critical condition. The ball went through her right lung, carrying with it pieces of cloth from her rubberized-cloth apron that was covered with juice and dirt from shucking the oysters. It traveled to her spine, where it was lodged. The surgeons probed and tried to remove it, but they were not successful. All they could do was to try to keep the wound as clean as possible while keeping Kate on a morphine drip for pain.

Back at the store, Lieutenant Hampton of the Twelfth Police District, along with other officers, searched the store and found the weapon hidden in the bin where Peter had placed it. It was a 0.38 caliber, seven-cylinder Colt revolver.

The police knew Peter McNally well from past family disturbances and complaints. They asked Kate's nephew James if he had seen where his grandfather went.

"He went across the street into the saloon," James replied.

Lieutenant Hampton went to the saloon. "I'm looking for Peter McNally."

"He was just here," the bartender said. "He came in, didn't say a thing. He bought a newspaper, folded it up, put it in his back pocket, and left, just a few minutes ago."

The officer left the saloon and scanned the streets.

He saw a man standing a few blocks away. He had a newspaper in his back pocket. Peter was arrested on Thompson Street near Eighth.

Lieutenant Hampton took Peter to the district station house, where he was booked. "Did you shoot your daughter?" he asked.

"Why no…but I suppose I could have," Peter replied.

Peter remained silent all the way to the station house and had a blank look on his face.

The police notified the family that he had been arrested and was being arraigned the next day.

At the arraignment, when asked about the incident, Peter said, "I am old and went down on my knees to beg for a home, then the devil got hold of me, I suppose." Peter said no more.

Magistrate Pullinger committed Peter to Moyamensing Prison to await the results of his daughter's injuries. He was immediately taken from the arraignment to the police wagon and about an hour's ride to Tenth and Wharton in South Philadelphia; he was to remain there, pending the fate of his daughter.

CHAPTER 19

1893–1894
Death and Trial

The doctors at St. Joseph's Hospital kept Kate on morphine to ease the extreme pain, although it was going to be a slow death because they could not remove the lead ball lodged in her spine.

A priest was called and gave Kate her last rights. Kate lapsed in and out of consciousness. Bridget spent the next five days at her daughter's bedside. Other family members visited, on and off, during the day and evening and brought their mother meals. On October 14th, just after midnight, a large full moon broke the southeastern horizon.

At this same time, miles to the south, Peter had been pacing in his prison cell. He couldn't sleep. As the moon arced upward into the Philadelphia sky, it illuminated the prison yard and threw its light through the bars of Peter's cell. It was a large orange moon, the same moon he was staring at the night before. This one seemed larger and almost to have a heartbeat as light wispy clouds passed in front of it, making it appear to be throbbing. He could almost hear the heartbeat of the moon.

Yes, it is a heartbeat. I can hear it...she's alive. She's alive, he thought hopefully, thinking of Kate as he stared at the moon. These thoughts were short-lived, however, as a sinking feeling soon spread through his entire being, and his perception of a heartbeat turned to silence, silence, except for the sound of a distant clock tower chiming midnight somewhere far to the north of the prison.

As dark black clouds quickly filled the sky, Peter's cell faded into total darkness. The wind picked up with a low howl beyond the prison walls as it blew through the surrounding buildings and trees.

Peter let out a loud cry, "Ahhhh!" Somehow, he knew Kate had died. Strangely, he did not shed a tear but simply turned and went into his prison bed, pulled up the blanket, and almost instantly fell asleep.

As he slept, the cloud cover moved away, and the Devil Moon cast its light through the barred prison window across Peter's sleeping face.

At the same time, just before midnight, Bridget fell asleep holding Kate's hand. The rising full moon shined into Kate's hospital room, washing her face with a reddish glow. She looked so at peace; it was midnight.

As the morning belfry chimes of St. Malachy rang in the new day, Kate took her last breath and slowly slipped away.

An hour later, Bridget was awakened by the early morning nurse, who told her that Kate was gone. The nurse watched as Bridget gently stroked Kate's cheek with the back of her hand, and with tears of grief, she kissed her forehead. The nurse pulled the sheet up over Kate's head. She helped Bridget to the hospital chapel on the first floor, where she waited for Agnes's usual morning visit at seven o'clock.

The hospital notified the local police district, and they ordered Peter to remain in custody at Moyamensing Prison until a trial date was set.

The *Philadelphia Times* published the following article:

FUNERAL OF A MURDERED WOMAN

A huge crowd gathered at the funeral of Katharine McNally, the young woman that was shot by her father, Peter McNally, at her home, Eleventh and Masters Streets, on Saturday last. The body lay in an open coffin in her home during the early hours of the morning and afterward taken to St. Malachi's, where a Solemn Requiem Mass was celebrated by the Reverend John Prendergast. Interment was subsequently made in the New Cathedral Cemetery. The pallbearers were John Swann, Charles Deeny, Thomas Hennessy, Tobias Schull, Kiernan Colgan, and John Inglenheiser, all members of St. Malachi's Church.[9]

After the funeral mass, the entourage drove in their carriages north to the New Cathedral Cemetery for the internment. It was a very long, slow ride, with many tears shed by family, church friends, and customers of the family store.

As the pallbearers carried the coffin to the grave site, it began to rain, light rain falling straight down on a windless day. The raindrops, like the tears of angels, fell on Kate's rose-covered coffin. Kate was buried next to her sisters Sallie, Angela Mary, and Genevieve.

The next day, the grocery store was open as usual, like nothing had happened. Bridget remained in her apartment for a whole month, not having the strength to face anyone but her children.

Bridget did not leave her room, not even for church. The parish priest came to visit her and, on one occasion, brought her communion.

Meanwhile, the warden at Moyamensing Prison informed Peter that his daughter had died, and he was to remain in solitary custody until his murder trial was scheduled. He sat in solitude, day and night, for five months. During this time, Joseph contacted a law firm to represent his father.

On more than one occasion, W. S. Furst and Maxwell Stevenson, attorneys, visited Peter. After asking similar questions on each visit and hearing varied answers, they were convinced he was mentally impaired, either a total lunatic or someone with advanced dementia. They prepared his defense based on those premises.

---

[9] *The Times*, Philadelphia, Pennsylvania, Saturday, October 21, 1893, page 9.

On Thursday, March 1, 1894, Peter paced in his prison cell. He had a restless night after the warden notified him that in the morning, he was being transferred to the Court of Oyer and Terminer for his trial. He already spoke to the attorneys his sons hired on his behalf and had been waiting some weeks for the day of the trial to begin. A prison guard brought him clothing that his son Edward brought to the prison for him to wear to the trial.

"Here, you'll need to change out of those prison clothes. Your son said it was the best he could find that you had. You'd look better in the prison clothes," said the guard with a chuckle.

After Peter changed, he was led to the prison wagon. It was a cloudy and frigid March morning. The guards opened up the rear doors of the wagon, helped Peter in, and handed him a blanket. There were benches on each side of the wagon, with only one small window in the rear door to allow some light in and another to allow the policeman next to the driver to observe the prisoner. They began the slow ride up Thirteenth Street.

As they drove on, his mind flashed in and out of reality at times, not knowing what this wagon was, why he was in it, or where it was going, to other very lucid moments with thoughts that he could be convicted of first-degree murder and go to the gallows within the week.

Peter could only see out the rear window. He watched the receding streetscapes. He hadn't seen a tree in four months, only the sky from the prison yard. The police wagon traveled up to Passyunk Avenue and then zigzagged the streets to the rear of the courthouse.

Peter had no idea where his trial was going to be held, but when he saw the State House, Independence Hall, he became frightened and felt very disoriented. The police wagon pulled up to the rear of the courthouse. Peter was escorted to a holding cell behind the courtroom. He didn't say a word, nor did the two policemen as they shut the iron-barred door with a clank and turned the key.

About thirty minutes later, his attorneys, W. S. Furst and Maxwell Stevenson, opened the door from the courtroom and walked the few steps to the holding cell.

Mr. Furst said, "Good morning, Mr. McNally, and we hope it will be a good morning for you. Do you remember us? We are the attorneys your family hired to represent you in this case. I'm W. S. Furst, and this is my partner Maxwell Stevenson."

Maxwell added, "We will do our very best for you, Mr. McNally, but you must realize the severity of the charge of murder. It is most grave, and your very life is at stake."

Peter looked stunned. He had a glazed-hypnotic look in his eyes and across his face.

"Are you all right, Mr. McNally? Did you understand what we are saying?" asked Mr. Stevenson.

Peter had been standing holding onto the cell bars, just staring at the men while they spoke to him. He finally moved his head very slowly up and down, still staring at his attorneys in silence for a long while.

"Mr. McNally, did you understand what we said to you?" repeated Stevenson.

Peter finally spoke in a low voice, "Yes."

"Your children are here to testify on your behalf. They will be doing all they can to save you from execution," said Furst. He continued, "The trial will start in about fifteen minutes. You will be ushered to the court dock by the state police who brought you here, and you will be asked to stand for the duration of today's trial. There will be some recesses during the course of the day for you to rest. Do you have the ability to stand?" asked Furst.

"Ah, I'm not sure. I...I don't think so," said Peter.

"We will request that the judge allow you to sit in the dock," said Furst.

Peter was led into the court dock, an iron-fence enclosure in the center of and near the front of the courtroom. It was about four feet high and four feet square, with an iron gate facing the courtroom front door. A chair had been placed in the dock for the prisoner. Peter walked in and sat down; the gate was closed and locked. The courtroom was crowded with all of Peter's children, a few other relatives, many curious spectators, and a few newspaper reporters filling the remainder of the seats.

One reporter for the *Philadelphia Times* quickly scribbled his first notes on his pad, "An old man, shabbily dressed, wild-eyed, with unkempt hair and beard, and a general air of neglect and hopelessness about him sat in the criminal dock of the Court of Oyer and Terminer...charged with murder."

The court clerk stood from his desk in front of the bench, turned and faced the courtroom, raised his hand, and announced loudly, "Quiet, please!" There was a quiet pause; the door to the judge's chambers opened, and the clerk proclaimed, "All rise, Oyez! Oyez! Oyez! The Honorable Judge Reed presiding."

Judge Reed walked swiftly to the bench, adjusted his robes, sat down, shuffled a few papers, slowly looked around the courtroom, then directly at the defendant. He struck his gavel. "This court is now in session."

Judge Reed was forty-six years old and descended from a long line of literary ancestors in addition to being a judge. He graduated from the University of Pennsylvania in 1865 and was admitted to the bar in 1869. He had been with the Commonwealth Court for almost twenty years but was not appointed to the high court until 1886.

During this six-year-plus tenure in the high court, he presided over many murder cases and followed the law to the letter, closely examining the testimonies and facts.

He was seemingly fair, yet in some circles, he was known as "The Hanging Judge."

The trial of the Commonwealth of Pennsylvania versus Peter David McNally began.

Peter's attorneys sat at a table, looking at the prosecution team representing the Commonwealth, awaiting their opening statements.

Instead, District Attorney Graham approached the defense counsel table and, in a whisper, offered a proposal, "Gentlemen, we can save a lot of time and offer to proceed with a guilty plea to a second-degree murder charge. If you change the plea to guilty of second-degree murder, we believe Judge Reed will allow you to proceed with your defense on that basis."

"And if our efforts fail to convince the judge, it should be second-degree murder, and he wants murder 1, then what?" asked Furst.

"We would then suggest that the defendant could withdraw his plea and be allowed a full jury trial if the judge decides on murder 1."

Furst and Maxwell looked at each other, both knowing the prosecution's depth of experience in trials like this and also knowing that their ability to convince the judge that Peter was insane at the time of the shooting was weak in having actual evidence. He did shoot her, and there were no other witnesses except for the young nephew. The accounts of doctors who examined Peter at different times a year before the shooting and who would be offering testimony today did not bare on, or relate to, his mental capacity on the actual day of the shooting. Furst and Maxwell nodded to each other and to the prosecutor. "We will accept the change of plea."

The next morning's edition of the *Philadelphia Times* described the reaction of the courtroom:

> A murmur of disappointment spread through the courtroom when District Attorney Graham, after a consultation with the prisoner's counsel, arose, addressing Judge Reed, who presided, said, "I ask Your Honor's attention to the case of the Commonwealth against Peter McNally charged with murder in shooting his daughter. The counsel for the prisoner desires permission for him to withdraw the plea of not guilty now on the record and substitute, therefore, a plea of guilty."[10]

District Attorney Graham continued with a long-drawn-out monologue, oozing with confusing, complex, complicated legalese.

Graham continued on and on with more and more boisterous legal rhetoric, pontificating his knowledge of the law.

---

[10] *Philadelphia Times*, March 2, 1894.

He paced slowly back and forth across the front of the courtroom with his chin raised, looking somewhat upward in an air of self-righteousness with only an occasional downward stare of disdain at the much younger McNally defense team.

Judge Reed was getting restless and finally interrupted the district attorney, "I believe you have made your point, Counselor." The judge continued, "Mr. Furst and Mr. Stevenson, are you agreeable to continue as the Commonwealth has so stated?"

Furst replied, "Our only concern is that our client's case might be seriously affected in that we would be disclosing all our defense for the benefit of the Commonwealth."

DA Graham argued on and on that the prosecution's offer was extremely fair and the only way the defendant could receive less than the death penalty.

The judge assured Peter's defense team that the proposition was very fair and had often been used in the past in similar cases.

"These proceedings will be purely formal, and your client's case will not be prejudiced in any way. Let me review the options as they are fairly straightforward. First, if you proceed with a not guilty plea and cannot support that through testimony, your client will be convicted of first-degree murder, which carries the death penalty. If a first-degree ruling is reached today, your client will have the right to a full jury trial. With a guilty plea to the murder, he has a chance of getting a second-degree conviction which would have an appropriate prison sentence. Did I make those options clear?"

"Yes, you did, Your Honor. We agree to proceed with the guilty plea," said Furst. With that, Judge Reed agreed to hear the evidence that morning.

All of Peter's children and relatives were in attendance, except for Bridget, and it was explained that all the children were afraid to bring her because it might be fatal, knowing her frail physical condition. She had been having heart problems.

After the judge made a few more remarks addressed to everyone in the courtroom, especially to witnesses, family and friends, and other curiosity-seeking attendees. He made it clear that there would be quiet and order in his court throughout the proceeding.

Lieutenant Hampton, the arresting officer, testified that he was called to the scene by the defendant's grandson, pointing to young James in the gallery and that he first tended to Catherine McNally while another officer ran for an ambulance. When asked if he spoke to the now-deceased Catherine McNally, he said, "Yes, I did, and I asked who shot her, and she said her father. After that, I spoke to young James Kelly, who said he saw his grandfather shoot his aunt Kate, and he told me that the defendant looked at the pistol he was holding and dropped it in a potato bin, and covered it with some paper. He then told me his grandfather walked out of the store and went into the saloon. That's all he saw."

The lieutenant went on as to how he tracked down the defendant in a matter of minutes and arrested him on the corner of Thompson and Eighth Streets. When he asked McNally why he had shot his daughter, Peter said he had raised a family of nine children, and they had deprived him of a home.

The prosecution called Detective Frank P. Geyer of the Twelfth Police District to testify. He identified a written sworn statement by the defendant on the evening of the shooting that stated, "I have no recollection of shooting my daughter."

James Kelly, Peter's grandson, now ten, was called as the only witness to the shooting. After his name was called to testify, Judge Reed said, "Young man, please come up here and have a seat next to me. You will first be asked to be sworn in with your hand on the Bible, just like the last witness, and then you will be asked some questions. Just answer them honestly and as completely as you can. If you don't know an answer, that's all right; just say so. Okay?"

"Yes, sir."

The prosecutor asked James if the man he was pointing to in the dock was his grandfather and if he saw him shoot his aunt Catherine. James said he did. Then the DA asked him what he saw that day. James described his grandfather coming into the store and asking his aunt to have his trunk taken upstairs. "She told him he had to leave, and he pulled out a gun and shot her. I ran out of the store and heard a second shot."

"Then what happened after the shooting stopped? Just tell me what you saw."

"After the shooting stopped, I looked back into the store and saw him put the pistol in the potato bin. Then he walked out and went across Master Street into the saloon."

The coroner's physician Henry L. Sidebotham followed with testimony that the cause of death of Catherine McNally was infection due to the gunshot wound. That closed the evidence for the Commonwealth.

The defense attorney Furst then said, "In order that all the light possible might be thrown on the case, we thought it advisable that the past life of the defendant should be brought to the attention of the court."

Furst told Peter's life story from his birth in Ireland, immigration to New York, and moving his family to Philadelphia, and all the grocery store business locations, along with the large family he supported. Then one by one, he called on Peter's four sons and two daughters to testify on their father's behalf. Each one recalled separate acts of apparent lunacy in the middle of the night when he was sure he heard someone trying to break into the store.

The stories were all very similar and covered all the store locations over the past years.

Agnes's testimony was probably the most compelling when she described his radical behavior "as more than mere eccentricities, but rather speech and actions the likes of a madman. He is a sick person."

On cross-examination, each of the sons and daughters was asked to give the timeframe of their testimony. The most recent was when their father was thrown out of the house after he came back drunk late at night. The DA asked Agnes, the last to testify, "That night, when your father returned to the house, you said 'drunk,' correct?"

"Yes, he was drunk."

"So, did he say or do anything a madman might say or do that night other than returning home drunk? Yes or no, please."

"Well, no."

"No further questions, Your Honor."

Furst then followed up on Agnes's testimony by calling the family doctor to testify.

Dr. S. Updegroves, the family physician, was called as an expert witness. He described that in the past years, the family expressed concern about Peter's mental stability, and at one point two years ago, his daughter Agnes thought he should be committed to an insane asylum. He concluded his testimony by saying, "The defendant had extreme dementia and often lost touch with reality."

On cross-examination, the prosecution asked Dr. Updegroves one question, "Do you know, as a fact, that on March 15, 1893, the day and time of the shooting, the defendant, Peter McNally, was out of touch with reality? Please answer yes or no, and let me remind you that you are under oath and subject to perjury."

Judge Reed sounded his gavel, "The Commonwealth shall refrain from issuing veiled threats to the witness. That is not appropriate in my court. Dr. Updegroves, please answer the question."

"The answer would have to be no."

"No further questions, Your Honor. The Commonwealth rests its case."

Judge Reed spoke, "The trial of the Commonwealth of Pennsylvania versus Peter D. McNally is now concluded. There will be a thirty-minute recess. During that time, I will review all testimonies and evidence for both parties. After which, the court will announce the verdict."

The gavel came down with a deafening thud.

"All rise!" The judge took his pile of written exhibits and his trial notes and walked swiftly to his chambers.

As soon as the chamber door closed, the courtroom became a heightened cacophony of simultaneous conversations.

The newspaper reporters had come in pairs, and with the recess, the junior reporter took all the trial stories and ran back to the editor so that the story could be written and edited for the morning's paper. The chief reporters remained for the verdict.

The undisciplined crowd was quickly silenced by the sergeant-at-arms. He loudly announced. "If I see you talking, you will be removed from this courtroom." The silence was instant.

The minutes going by seemed like hours for the family. Thirty minutes went by, then forty, then fifty. The door to the judge's chambers finally opened at four o'clock after an hour recess.

"All rise! The court of the Honorable Judge Reed is now back in session."

Judge Reed asked the defendant, who had been given permission to sit through the trial, to stand up and face the bench.

Two armed state policemen stood, one on each side of the dock. The judge opened a folder and removed one piece of paper, studied it for a moment, almost the time to proofread the verdict.

"The Commonwealth of Pennsylvania, after careful examination of all evidence and testimony, hereby finds the defendant, Peter David McNally, guilty of murder in the second degree and is hereby sentenced to twenty years in state prison."

All sorts of gasps and shouts rang out from the courtroom gallery.

The judge sounded his gavel three times loudly and told everyone in the courtroom to remain silent in their seats until the prisoner was removed. The judge exited the courtroom first and returned to his chambers.

Peter was led from the dock to the exit door at the front of the courtroom. He didn't look at anyone, just at the floor. The policemen escorted him out the same door he came in and onto the waiting horse-drawn carriage. He was on his way, not back to Moyamensing Prison, where the gallows were waiting, but to Eastern State Penitentiary on Fairmont Avenue, only seven blocks south of the scene of the murder. This was to be his home for the next twenty years.

When the rear door closed, the courtroom broke into a pandemonium of maundering chatter. A reporter from *The Times* rushed toward the McNally family, who were just standing from their seats and trying to exit the building.

"Mr. McNally," the reporter called to Joseph, the oldest of the men, "Do you have any comments on today's verdict?"

Joseph raised his voice, "Step back and let my family by! Step back, please," dodging the question. "Go on now, get back!"

The young reporter sensed Joseph's anger, and seeing his size; he wanted no part of an argument.

James said goodbye to the group and headed east to his saloon. Joseph and Agnes led the procession down Chestnut Street to Eleventh. They could have waited for the trolley but needed the walk after the long day of sitting in the courtroom. It was a frigid day with a lot of hard-packed snow and ice on the sidewalks and streets. The walk was slow going to the trolley stop, but the wait there was short. Both the walk and ride were silent.

When the trolley stopped at Master Street, next to O'Connor's Saloon, Agnes told her brothers she was going to see mother and tell her the results and stay with her. Bridget's nerves had been on edge ever since Kate was shot and later died. She was in a very fragile condition.

The McNally men went into the saloon. When they entered, the noisy bar became hushed, with all eyes looking toward the door.

"Well," said Joseph, "Father did not fare well in court. We all tried to tell the judge that our father had lost his mind. I think you all know that and have seen it too. No use hiding across the street. You are all our friends and neighbors, and for us now, life has to go on. Father got twenty years in prison." They were all still in silence, just holding their half-empty beer mugs. "Well, that's how it went, and now all we can do is buy you all another round."

And with that, there was applause and cheers. The McNallys milled around in the bar crowd, talking to different friends.

Agnes went upstairs, where Bridget had been sewing a dress all day as the store was closed. When Agnes entered, Bridget was in her rocking chair. She looked up, and when she saw Agnes's face, she knew it did not go well for Peter. She had a blank look on her face showing no emotion except quiet withdrawal.

"He got twenty years."

Bridget put her needle in the spool of thread on the table next to her, looked at Agnes, and said, "I'm all right. Actually, I'm much better now. We shall all have twenty years of peace."

CHAPTER 20

Family Post Trial Years
1894–1900

As the days went by, everyone was better off with Peter in prison. They all continued with their daily jobs.

PJ was twenty and still enjoying his job both as a master engraver and a plate printer at Charles Elliott and Sons Printing and Engraving Company. His boss, Everett Schmitz, who had no children, became very attached to Peter. They had similar personalities and got along like father and son. Peter spent much of his home time, on the weekends, at the Schmitz home a few blocks away. He always had his Sunday dinner there and spent holiday time there as well. He never felt very close to his mother and was afraid of his father, and he really didn't relate to many of his brothers and sisters. As somewhat of a loner, he was the luckiest of the lot, staying away from what had been a constant family drama.

The family did have some concerns about Peter's incarceration, as there had been articles in the newspapers that the state of Pennsylvania was considering letting certain inmates at Eastern State Penitentiary out early for good behavior because of extreme crowding conditions. There had been several small articles in the newspapers.

Bridget thought, *Oh, please, Lord, don't let him be good. Keep him bad, like he was here, so he'll stay there.* With Peter now in prison, Agnes returned to work full-time at the bakery, helping her husband.

Edward took over Kate's job in managing the store. Joseph quit his job at Baldwin Locomotive Works to help Edward at the store.

He did all the store purchasing at the Reading Terminal Market. Occasionally, on Sundays, Edward would ask PJ to go with Joseph, but PJ hated to go because even though he was a brother, PJ, in many ways, could not stand him. He didn't like that his brother was always bragging about what a tough guy he was. Joseph's tough-guy image often caused him to end up in fisticuffs with someone.

One day, when Joseph was returning from the usual Tuesday shopping trip, along with the produce and other foodstuffs, he had a bundle of newspapers he bought for the store and a smaller bundle for Tommy O'Connor's saloon across the street.

It was April 12, and the headline on the front page only had one word in large capital letters, "War."

In April of 1898, the United States declared war on Spain. The United States Navy battleship *Maine* was sunk on February 15 in Havana harbor. The battle cry was "Remember the *Maine*, to hell with Spain!" Plenty of volunteers stepped forward, including James and Joseph, but neither of the McNally men was chosen, as over seventy thousand volunteers had already enlisted.

To the McNallys and other Philadelphia families who did not have a relative in the war, it was merely interesting reading in the daily newspapers.

That same day, April 12, Edward took a copy of *The Times* upstairs for his mother to read the news about the war. She did and continued to read the local news. When she got to page ten, her eyes were drawn to the feature article headline:

Lunatics' Fatal Fray

One Philadelphia Hospital Patient Takes the Life of Another
He Gave Peter McNally the Fatal Blow

The reason why the killing of Peter McNally by Bernard O'Toole in Philadelphia Hospital was not made public until yesterday [and] was not explained by Superintendent Lawrence or resident physician Hughes. It was a very exciting murder, seen by at least a score, and the officials evidently spent a good deal of the time, at the expense of the city, in temporarily quieting the matter...

The article went on that the scene was the receiving ward of the Insane Unit. O'Toole was an epileptic and had been hospitalized there numerous times. His principal indication of insanity was, as often repeated by him, a declaration that he was the champion boxer of the world. The resident physician and all the staff knew him well and were supposed to keep an unusually close watch on him, but for some unknown reason, they did not that morning.

Peter McNally had been admitted several months before with extreme senile dementia. He had a fall and fractured a few ribs. On this morning, he was standing by his bed, looking out the window, when O'Toole walked into the ward and, upon spotting Peter, charged with a clenched fist and delivered a blow to the head. Peter fell to the floor by the side of his bed and never regained consciousness. He died several hours later from a brain hemorrhage.

When Bridget read the first line of the story and saw Peter's name, she let out a loud scream, the same type of scream as when Kate was shot. She dropped her cup on the table, breaking the saucer. Her hands flew up and covered her face. "Jesus, Mary, and Joseph!" she cried.

"Mother, what's wrong?" hollered Edward from the next room. He ran in to see what was wrong.

At first, she was speechless, just grabbing the paper in her clenched fist, and with tears rolling down her cheeks, she thrust the paper up toward Edward.

"This!"

Edward had a puzzled look on his face until his eyes focused on the story. "Jesus! Jesus!" He dropped the paper to the floor, dropped to his knees in silence, and hugged his mother, who was still sitting in the chair. They both were in shock.

Neither spoke for a long while. Edward finally said, "Get up, Mother. We both need to talk about this. Let's go into the other room. I will clean up the tea later."

Finally, the shock of the news was replaced by the simple reality: Bridget's husband, Edward's father, was dead. It was over. They figured that the prison must have sent Peter to the mental ward at the hospital after finally realizing his condition.

When they told the others in the family, they had the same reaction. Their minds were a blur for several days as they talked with each other, including James, who was still running his saloon. Edward told the family he would go to Oliver Blair, the family funeral director, and have him pick up the body, and he would make the arrangements for a burial other than in the family plot. He picked out a coffin, made the arrangements for transportation for the only family member who wanted to attend, left a deposit, and went back to the store. Later that same day, the funeral director stepped into the store, looking very perplexed. Edward, who was busy doing stock inventory, looked surprised by the visitor. He said, "Yes, Oliver, what is it?"

"He was already picked up by someone this morning, and they said they were not privileged to tell me who, only family."

"What? I don't understand."

"I don't either, but there is nothing I can do except cancel the arrangements and return your deposit. There will be no charge for my time. I'm sorry, Edward."

Edward checked the other newspapers to see if there were more details or other people mentioned or where he might have been living before going into the hospital, all with no luck. He even went and spoke with the newspaper reporter at *The Times*, who said that there was no more information than he had written in the story.

Edward went to the Philadelphia Hospital and spoke to admissions and asked who brought his father in for admission. After showing his identification and telling the admissions nurse that Peter was his father, she said, "Oh, I am very sorry," and she opened her files.

"He walked in here by himself two weeks ago, apparently knowing he was in trouble mentally, and checked himself in. He had enough money to cover the first month here, so he was admitted. The admissions doctor's notes say he was in and out of reality."

"Well, who claimed his body?" Edward asked.

"It was Riley's down on Dickinson Street," she said and showed Edward the name and address.

"Was a family member there to identify the body?" Edward asked.

"Yes, it was his brother James. See here; he signed the register. His brother was discussing cremation with the undertaker. That's all I know."

Edward looked and saw that it was signed by James McNally in very shaky handwriting. Edward thought James must have been in shock like they were. He lowered his head and gave a big exhale while shaking his head. He thanked the nurse and left. Before going to the trolley stop, he walked to James's saloon to thank him for taking care of things. When he arrived, the bartender told him James had left that morning and would be gone all day. Edward thanked him and walked to the Eleventh Street trolley.

On the way home, he put together what must have happened. They had been reading in the papers that the state penitentiary was considering early releases, and that's what must have happened, and they missed seeing anything in the paper. He knew his father at his worst and knew he was crazy, so he must have had a touch of reality, which he often did, and checked himself into the hospital since he had no place else to go. After he was murdered, James must have read the same story and, being the only family who ever had a decent relationship with him, must have arranged for cremation, knowing the family would not have him buried at New Cathedral. It all made sense.

When he got back to the store, he gathered everyone and gave the explanation. What had been a mystery was now solved. Peter was dead. That was that, and James dealt with it for them. There was nothing else to do.

The next day, they just seemed to have shrugged it off and got back to business as usual in running the store. After that incident, not one of them ever mentioned Peter's name again nor spoke of the murder to anyone, nor did any of their customers, their priest, any of the local police, the neighbors, or even the postman or bartender.

The neighborhood was changing fast. Older families had died or moved. Many Irish families moved to South Philadelphia into several Irish enclaves; thus, most of the loyal customers of the McNally grocery were no more.

New younger families moved into the Germantown residences and into the growing Northern Liberties section of the city to the north.

The trolley schedules were adjusted to provide more trolleys to serve the populous of the growing northern city, taking them to and from the city center to the stores, businesses, and the ever-growing Reading Terminal Market. The McNally business was drying up at the same rapid pace.

Agnes, Joseph, and Edward were the only family members who stayed with the store. They did well and saved most of their profits, except for the few recreational splurges they made over the years, including one extravagant trip, by train, to the Baldwin Hotel in Beach Haven on Long Beach Island at the New Jersey Shore for two weeks in 1898.

Eventually, the family celebrated the beginning of a new century. They were all in agreement that it was time to close the grocery store for good. They all had a decent bankroll of savings, and each was ready to make this major change.

Unbeknownst to all of them, Peter McNally, the family patriarch, was also ushering in the new century in his cell at Eastern State Penitentiary. Some other Peter McNally was killed, as reported in *The Times* article. The brother James, who picked up the body at Philadelphia Hospital, was the deceased's brother, coincidentally, with the name "James." None of the McNally family would ever know this truth.

CHAPTER 21

Prison Life
1884–1902

As the police wagon transporting Peter headed north on Ninth Street and turned west on Fairmount Avenue, there it was, the towering stone walls of this castle-like prison, Eastern State Penitentiary, covering two city blocks and appearing to have been dropped into the middle of the surrounding three-story brick residential neighborhood.

When the wagon neared the massive entrance gate, the smaller man-door in the main gate opened, and a guard stepped out. He motioned the driver to pull the wagon up to the smaller door. Peter was handcuffed behind his back and was assisted in getting out of the wagon and led through the door into the space inside the main gate. The front door was shut and locked behind him. Only then was the inside door of the main gate opened into the front prison yard. He would not see the streets of Philadelphia again for many years to come. He glanced up at the late afternoon sky; a small gray first-quarter waxing moon was in the sky; he was not to see the moon again for the next twenty years either nor the sun. His cell faced to the north with no views of the sun or the moon ever.

He was led across the prison yard into the receiving area where he was received, and handcuffs were removed. He was assigned inmate number A 7328. A wooden placard, painted white, with his stenciled inmate number in black, was hung around his neck. After which, the prison photographer took his mug shots.

The state police gave the prison reception personnel the sentencing information from the court, along with a box of Peter's possessions that were taken from him when he was arrested in October. He was interviewed, measured, and weighed, and then he was changed into prison clothes. His street clothes were added to the box of possessions and filed in a storage room. Then Peter was led to Warden Cassidy's office.

Cassidy served in cellblock three as overseer until 1870, when he became the penitentiary deputy warden and was later promoted to warden.

The president of inspectors, Andrew Malone, described Cassidy as "a great reader, an educated man, a man of very great mental power and strength of character."[11]

The receiving officer gave the workhouse record to the warden. He looked it over and then looked up at Peter, who looked as frightened as could be.

"Sit down, Mr. McNally," said the warden. "You will be getting to know me quite well, as one of my jobs is to speak with every prisoner every day as my time permits. You should know that I am not at all concerned about any of the details of your crime, but I want you to know I am concerned about you and your rehabilitation here at ESP, your physical health, mental and spiritual status. We here at ESP try very hard to work as a family, an unusual one, I admit, but a good one. All the inmates get a job to do. It's good for them, and we need workers so that we can be self-sufficient. We have our own gardens and greenhouse. We grind our own flour and make our own bread. We have a tailor shop and leatherworks shop, where we make our own clothing, boots, and shoes, and many items for sale on the outside, so there are lots for everyone to do. We even have our own barbershop if your hair or beard needs a trim from time to time.[12] We are here to help you. I see on your record sheet that you were a grocer and used to be a Moroccan finisher. What exactly is that trade? Can you tell me?"

---

[11] Paul Kahan, Eastern State Penitentiary, A History.
[12] Ibid.

Peter spoke in a quiet voice, "When I was young, back in Ireland, I worked with my father at a tannery, tanning goatskins. It was called Morocco finishing. The leather was used to bind expensive books."

"Well, about the only thing we don't have here is a book bindery, although we do have a printing plant. With your experience in the grocery business, it seems you would be suited to work in the commissary. They need extra hands there, and they will teach you our process of ordering and dispensing foodstuff and supplies to various areas of the prison. So now we have a job for you."

Peter didn't quite know what to make of all that the warden was saying. It was not so much what he said but how he said it. It was said in a very different tone from the last words he heard from the judge, which was quite a tongue-lashing as his sentence was read. Peter sat in silence and listened to the warden.

"Peter, this officer will take you to meet your cellblock officer for cellblock three, my old stomping ground. You will have adequate quarters there, and you will be expected to maintain the cleanliness and order of your cell at all times in the condition it is in now. Is that clear?"

"Yes."

"Good then. Officer Jenkins will take you now. You'll not have a cellmate as yet, till we see how you acclimate to life here at ESP. Your cellblock gets the call to breakfast at six-thirty, lunch at twelve-thirty, and dinner at six o'clock. Here, take this booklet and read it. It tells you our rules here, which must be obeyed, and it tells you of your rights here. It also lists all the activities available for you, and, of course, the restrictions listed apply to everyone. Follow the rules, and life here will be tolerable. You are dismissed. I will speak with you again sometime tomorrow. Welcome to ESP." And with that, he extended his hand.

Peter stood up from the chair, shook the warden's hand, and was led to his cell. His twenty-year sentence had just begun.

On day one, Peter was led to his cell and told to lower his head, and with the guard's hand on top of it, he was told to stoop down and to walk ahead slowly. He was in his new home for the next twenty years (7,300 days)!

The prison was massive, with high stone fortress-like walls. There were eight spoke-like cell blocks, long corridors with cells on each side on two levels. The cell blocks radiated from a central point, a rotunda, where one guard could observe down the long corridors by simply turning his head.[13]

The cells had a metal door to the cellblock corridor, purposely designed low so as to prevent a prisoner from dashing out when a guard opened it. Each cell was eighteen feet deep and eight feet wide, with a tall ceiling. The walls were eighteen-inch thick, reinforced concrete. There was a metal grill door at the back of the cell that led to a personal recreation yard for each cell. It was about the same size as the cell and had such a high wall that no one could escape over it, and if they did, it would be into a secured space within the prison walls.

There was a metal bed with a thin mattress and a wool blanket, along with a concrete toilet, a wash sink, and a few small cloths for washing. Prisoners were allowed to add decorations or pictures in their cells and even furniture.[14]

At first, he had no contact with the outside world other than his walled-in exercise area outside of his prison cell on the north side of the prison.

The view was limited to the sky overhead. He was lucky to see a few clouds. Because of the location of his exercise yard, on the north side of the prison, he could not see the sun or the moon, ever, nor the stars, for he was not allowed to go there at night. A few months after his admission, he was permitted to go to the prison library for an hour a week, where he could read books or newspapers. He would do this on Sunday mornings after breakfast.

Depending on what was going on in adjoining cells, from time to time, he was led to and from his cell in cellblock three by the guard to the prisoner's mess or the library. The guard would put a hood put over his head so he could not see what was going on in other parts of his environment.

---

[13] Paul Kahan, Eastern State Penitentiary, A History.
[14] Ibid.

Peter enjoyed working in the prison commissary because he had company to talk to, and the work was interesting and varied. One day, he would be packaging food and produce on delivery carts for the prison kitchen; on other days, he would unpack materials for the various prison shops: leather for the cobbler shop, wheat for the bakery, where they ground their own flour, and ink, paper, and other supplies for the print shop.

Many of the prisoners who had been making shoes and items like furniture or leather goods for the market outside of the prison eventually lost their jobs due to union objections to the prison-made goods, which were sold on the outside market. The prison shoes and boots were better than the union-made ones and cost less, so it was a threat that needed to be stopped, and the state democratic party stopped it.

As the new century approached, the once successful rehabilitation work method of the Pennsylvania penal system was caving in due to continuing union and political pressure. Fortunately for Peter, this did not affect his work at the prison commissary.

The warden came to speak with Peter almost every day in his early years at the prison, even if briefly, and all the other prisoners as well, which was part of his job. As the prison population grew to a crowded condition, the warden's daily visits became less and less.

The "Prisoner's Rights" booklet told Peter what he could and could not do, mainly what he could not do. It told him to ask his cellblock officer if he had any questions. Peter did ask if there was a priest he could see.

"Yes, we have a prison chaplain. I will arrange for your cellblock officer to set up a visitation schedule."

The next morning after the warden's visit, Peter was having breakfast in the prisoners' mess. A fight broke out between two of the inmates. One of the prisoners, holding his dining fork, lunged at the other's face. The second fellow reached out and grabbed his attacker by the beard, gave it a twist, and dragged the man's face down into the edge of the dining table, dislodging several of the attacker's teeth. Guards came in and broke up the ruckus. Both men were taken away, and each was put in solitary confinement. Peter did not see them again for two weeks. The men never fought again.

The day after the fight, the warden stopped by Peter's cell for a brief visit. Warden Cassidy called for the guard to open the cell.

"Do you have any questions for me today, Mr. McNally?"

"Yes, can I get my beard cut shorter?"

"Of course. I will advise your cellblock officer, who will arrange for that. Is there anything else?"

"No, sir."

As he was leaving, the sweet sound of violin music, one violin, reverberated throughout the cellblock and into Peter's cell, which added to the often-contradictory illusions of his new world. The prison regulations, under Warden Cassidy, allowed any prisoner to possess a musical instrument and play it between 6:00 a.m. and 10:00 p.m. The instrument could be anything from a Jew's harp to a piano. The prisoner or his family had to provide the instrument.[15]

Above the main cellblock was a gallery, or second floor of cells, accessed by stairs. Access to those cells was by walkways on each side of the gallery. The walkways, with railings, were open overlooking the first floor of the cellblock.

To Peter McNally, the only change he saw in his first four years was the addition of a cellmate after six months of living alone in his cell. It was a welcome change. The new prisoner was a young Russian, also convicted of murder. His sixteen-year-old sister was raped by a twenty-six-year-old blacksmith. Victor went to the blacksmith shop, came behind the man, and smashed his skull with a hammer. There were three witnesses.

Victor's thoughts that justice was served were dashed when he learned he killed the twin brother of the rapist. The victim was survived by a wife and three young children.

The Russian, Victor Denisovich, was just twenty-one years old, and like Peter, he had been sentenced to twenty years for murder in the second degree. His crime was judged a crime of passion without the intent of murder.

---

[15] Paul Kahan, Eastern State Penitentiary, A History.

Victor spoke fairly good English, and the two got along well. The company was good for Peter, as his early visits with the priest were not helping him at all, other than fanning the flames of guilt for his crime. The prison chaplain kept trying to get Peter to atone for the mortal sin of shooting his daughter, while Peter kept saying he never remembered shooting her. He kept saying, "The devil must have got in me," and that was what he believed.

On the fourth visit from the chaplain, Peter said, "Father, I don't want to see you anymore. Go and spread your joy somewhere else."

"But, Peter, I don't understand."

"What is it about 'Go away' that you don't understand? Goodbye, Father." And he turned his back.

The years rolled by. Over the years, the days were all the same, except, on a rare Sunday, Peter would attend chapel and sit in the back row. Once a week, he was allowed to visit the library. He liked to read *The Philadelphia Times* and keep up with what the world was doing outside, a world he could not imagine he would ever see again. Twenty years was going to be a long time.

On April 12, 1898, Peter paid his usual Sunday late morning visit to the library to read the newspaper. The headline on the front page only had one word in large capital letters, "WAR."

The United States declared war on Spain. The United States Navy battleship, USS *Maine*, was sunk on February 15 in Havana harbor. The US reaction was tantamount to someone must be blamed; someone will be punished. That seemed to be the big news of the day, but when Peter got to page 10, his eyes were drawn to the feature article headline and the story that followed:

LUNATICS' FATAL FRAY

One Philadelphia Hospital Patient Takes the Life
of Another
He Gave Peter McNally the Fatal Blow

Peter read the story. The article did not give details about where the victim lived or information about the victim's family. Peter instantly thought this was about his son, PJ.

"Oh my god! He killed my son. My PJ is gone!" He always knew PJ was not talkative with him, thinking he was just shy and not thinking he could have been deeply depressed or had the beginnings of dementia.

The devil is killing my family, one by one, he thought. He slumped with grief over the library table and cried for the second time ever in his life. He grieved over his son's death for months. After that day, when he returned to the library to read, he read magazine articles, but never again the paper, as he was afraid there might be details of the trial, which would only magnify his grief.

Over the next four years, life in prison was the same routine, day after day, week after week. The only escape he had from the boredom was in his mind, and that usually was not a good place for him to go.

The lack of stress, a nutritional diet, regular exercise, and casual conversations with his cellmate and other inmates seemingly was a cure to his deep mood swings.

He thought a lot about Kate and wondered what it was that brought him to shoot her. *How could I do that?* He would think. All he could think of was, *It must be a spell cast on me by that Devil Moon.*

With all his failures and the tragedies in his life, the Devil Moon was there, piercing his soul and seemingly controlling his actions. He had not seen the Devil Moon in eight years. He felt safe now, protected from the spell. He was reasonably content.

CHAPTER 22

Free at Last
1900–1910

By 1900, there were all sorts of investigations into the activities and management of Eastern State Penitentiary, many fueled by the labor unions and the state democrats. Warden Cassidy hated the investigations and questioning. This was his prison; how dare they. The population at ESP was causing overcrowded conditions because of an explosion in crime following the Civil War, long sentences for many serious crimes, and a growing population that yielded more and more convicts. By 1900, there were nearly two thousand inmates. Overcrowding forced the administration to add more cells, which created a problem: how would they fit those cells into a prison where the architecture was part of the security system? The administrators and architects modified the prison as best they could.[16]

There was also some relief when the federal government decided in 1902 to remove all the prisoners housed in Eastern State Penitentiary.[17]

Other state prisoners were also released early for good behavior if they were deemed not a threat to society. This purging would take place not all at once but phased over the year.[18] Inmate No. A7328

---

[16] Paul Kahan, Eastern State Penitentiary, History.
[17] Ibid.
[18] Ibid.

was about to see the streets of Philadelphia once again and the sun and the moon, twelve years ahead of schedule.

By March 1902, Peter McNally had been in ESP for eight years. The facility was overcrowded. Peter was not a troublemaker nor thought to be a threat to society. He was one the first on the release list.

About three days after his eighth year in ESP, on the occasion of the warden's visit, the warden said, "Peter, I have some good news for you."

Peter stood up from his bed where he was resting and came to the bars of his cell. He stooped down to look out through the barred cell door and looked at the warden, who was smiling. "Peter, tomorrow morning, you are being released. You will be a free man. You have been an exemplary inmate. You have played by the rules, and you are now ready for early release. You will be released after breakfast tomorrow at ten o'clock. Congratulations."

With that, the warden extended his hand through the bars. Peter looked at it and didn't know what to do. He didn't reach out to shake his hand. He just stood there with a blank look on his face, looking at the warden.

Peter finally spoke, "But, Warden, what will I do? This is my home. I have no place to go."

"Peter, I'm sorry, but we need to make room in this institution for new prisoners, and you are on the official list to be released. I'll see you in the morning. I'll make sure you have sufficient funds to get you on your way, but for now, try to get a good rest. I'll see you tomorrow after breakfast." The warden turned and left.

Peter tossed and turned all night, thinking about where he would go and what he would do. He had become so accustomed to the regular schedule in prison. He had met other inmates who became what he considered friends. He wouldn't see them anymore. He had no friends on the outside other than James, his brother. What would he do? Where would he go? He had no job waiting for him, no place to stay, and no answers.

Peter lay there awake for what seemed like several hours, mulling over all these thoughts, which eventually gave way to sleep.

With the morning wake-up call at five o'clock, Peter got up, left his cell at six o'clock, and walked in formation with the third group from cellblock 3 to the male gang shower.

While showering, one of the prisoners he knew but didn't like, Antonio Vitable, was watching him shower. Peter was well built for his age. He had been doing push-ups in his exercise yard for eight years, lifting his iron bed to do weight curls, which gave him a muscular build with massive biceps. Peter always thought Vitable was a homo, and that's what the inmates called him "Tonio, the homo."

Tonio said, "Are you getting out today, McNally?" continuing to watch Peter soap up his armpits and biceps.

"Yea, what's it to you, homo?" Seeing Tonio's obvious lecherous, concupiscent gaze, Peter clenched both his jaw and his fist and flexed his bicep and said, "Don't even think about it, homo, unless ya want a fat lip." When he clenched his jaw, he felt a somewhat painful twinge all along the right side of his jaw. He hadn't noticed that before, but he had not clenched his teeth that hard before, even when eating; he passed it off, not giving it a second thought; the sensation went away.

One inmate said, "Go for it, Pete. It's lonely out there, you know." The inmates in the shower room all broke out in hilarious laughter.

Peter left the shower, got dressed, and went to breakfast. There he talked with a few of the friends he had made over the years, telling them that he was leaving. They said they would miss him and wished him good luck and that they were all leaving over the next months, and maybe they could catch up with him somewhere on the outside.

When breakfast was finished, the dining room supervisor told Peter to come with him to the warden's office. Warden Cassidy was expecting Peter, along with a few other inmates. Peter was the first in line, as he had been at ESP the longest time.

"Well, now, Peter, you have the honor of being first. It's time for you to be released and for you to get back into society."

Peter just stood there. "But where will I go? I have no place to go. My family won't take me back. Where will I go? This is my home."

"Well, Peter, I understand, but you have no choice. There must be someone, a friend, who could help you. Where did you go to the last time you needed someone to help you?"

Peter thought for a minute. It was long ago before prison. "Why, I suppose that would be my brother, James. James helped me in the past. He did come and visit me in the first few years here. I suppose his life has moved on, but I may be able to find him."

"Peter, that being the case, I suggest you go see your brother. Is he in the city?"

"Yes, I believe he still is. He has a saloon on South Second. I'm not sure he's still there, but I'll go there and see."

"I know this release came suddenly and might be a frightful thought for you after being here for eight years, and what with being accustomed to our daily routine, but you will do fine on the outside. You're a new man now, Peter. You've done well here. You've been respected by other inmates and all the staff, and me. I wish you God's speed, and I have some advice for you. If there are those who were involved in your incarceration eight years ago, it's my sincere advice not to seek them out. Just let the past be the past. Let it drift away. Don't revisit it."

And with that, the warden said, "I'm returning the possessions you had when you came here." He opened a box that had the things he was wearing when admitted, a worn pair of gray linen trousers, a collared shirt, and wool sox. These had been washed in the prison laundry, anticipating his release. There was a pair of old boots with holes in the soles and an envelope. The warden opened the envelope and poured into his hand a nickel and a penny, 6 ¢, the only money Peter had on him at the time of his arrest.

Peter was told to go into a changing room to change out of his prison garb and back into his street clothes. It was winter and freezing outside, so he was also given a regulation ESP winter jacket on which the "ESP Prisoner" stencil had not yet been placed. He was also allowed to wear his prison boots. The warden asked if he wanted to take his old ones with him. He said no.

"Peter, you are officially no longer an inmate of ESP. I wish you the best as you reenter society." The warden stood, walked to the front of his desk extended his hand and offered him an envelope. As was the case, the Commonwealth gave each departing inmate $50 cash in small bills to which the warden added five, five-dollar bills of his own. He had the practice of doing that for certain inmates with whom he felt some sort of relationship. Peter was escorted to the front gate and walked out onto the sidewalk of Fairmont Avenue a free man, but was he?

It was a cold, damp March morning. Peter knew exactly where he was, being familiar with the neighborhood, as his store was only a few blocks to the northeast.

He did not, however, follow the warden's advice. Instead, almost by instinct and out of extreme curiosity, he walked east on Fairmont Avenue, then north on Eleventh, just a few blocks to Master Street. When he was approaching the intersection, he saw the building on the corner. The familiar green awning was gone. All that was left was the iron bar frame for the awning. All the first-floor windows and front door windows were boarded up. The attached apartment on Eleventh Street had a "For Rent" sign on the door.

Peter looked across the street. The saloon was still there but now had a different name, "Blarney Stone Irish Pub." He walked in. There was a new bartender he didn't recognize, nor did he recognize any of the patrons at the bar. He approached the unfamiliar bartender and asked his name.

"Why, I'm John McNeil. I work for the owner, Tommy O'Connor." Peter asked the bartender when the store across the street closed and if he knew where the McNallys moved. The bartender said he was new at the pub. "All I know is they closed, and they all moved out last year."

"I'm new here too, and I never got to know any of them," said one of the barflies.

Peter left and walked east to Ninth Street and, on the way, saw no one he knew. He walked a block further to Kroberger's Grocery; it was still there and open. He went in. There was a young man behind the meat counter.

"Excuse me, is Kro about?"

"I'm sorry, he passed away three years ago. I'm his son, Raulfh. Can I help you?"

"Oh, I'm sorry, well no, I suppose not. I was an old friend of his and hadn't seen him for some time. I used to have a store in the neighborhood. Kro and I were good friends."

Peter walked out and waited for the southbound trolley. On the ride downtown, he looked at the neighborhoods and buildings, and stores. They all looked vaguely familiar; Peter's dementia was getting worse in spite of the eight years of healthy living in prison. He also had not seen the moon for eight years.

He got off the trolley at South Street and walked east. His brother's saloon was still there. He walked through the front door. There were only three people at the bar, chatting and sipping beer. When Peter walked in, James looked up. At first, he didn't recognize his brother, who always had a full beard and mustache but now was clean-shaven. But when Peter said, "James, it's me, Peter, your brother," James immediately recognized his voice and then saw his eyes and yelled, "Jesus, Mary, and Joseph, 'dag magadlh at'at'u [an Irish slang, meaning I'm very surprised]! Pete, what in the name of the saints are you doing here?"

"I was released today and went looking for the family, but they're all gone, and the store is closed."

"Well, Pete, after you went away, I saw the family less and less. They all had their things to do, their own lives, and I had mine. You know, we were only close the first year or so you were here and when I helped you move to your first store. I guess that's just the way it is with large families. I have no idea where they all went, and none of them came here to see me. Well, listen, I read in the paper last month that they were letting everyone out sometime this year but had no idea when or that you were out."

With that, James came from behind the bar and gave Peter a big hug, grabbing him by the shoulders and giving him a loving shake.

"Pete, so good to see you. You look so good. How the hell are ya now?"

Peter explained that he was released this morning and how he went to the store and found it closed and that no one was living in the apartments.

James said, "You remember when I last visited you? I told you I finally got married to a real nice girl, Sally. We have two kids, Joe, six, and Sophia Mae, four."

"Sorry, I don't remember. My memory is slipp'n a bit now."

"Ya don't? Well, it was a long time ago when I visited you anyway. We live on South Second; I bought a nice two-story brick house there. It's very close to the saloon. So, Pete, how can I help ya?"

"Well, I got no place to stay."

"Well, you can stay here in my old room in the back. It still has the bed, blankets, and a pillow. I still have that old galvanized tub. Rarely do I use the room now, maybe to take a nap or if I'm 'in the doghouse,'" he said with his telltale laugh. "But, Pete, this can only be temporary till you find work and get a job and a place to stay. So walk around the neighborhood, and see how things have changed, but first things first, let me get you something to eat and get you set up in your room. Then, why don't ya take a walk and have a look? Then later I'll take ya to meet my family. Tomorrow, I'll bring you breakfast, and you can look some more and maybe find a job."

With all the years in prison, Peter had become a creature of habit. He woke up at five-thirty, did his exercises, ate his breakfast at seven, then worked at the commissary till five-thirty, dinner at seven, and lights out at nine-thirty. He did have an hour off once a week when he spent time in the library reading.

The only thing he had missing now was a job, and it left him with an empty feeling, almost a panic, over that one missing thing in his schedule.

For days, he roamed the streets, looking for work, walking in different directions on different streets.

One morning, he decided to walk west on Market Street. There was no work at the street markets. He tried, but they were all owner-vendors with family help.

He walked past Snellenburg's, which he didn't remember as a small dry goods store when he opened his first store on Sixth

Street. Well, it wasn't small anymore. It was a tall six-story building taking up almost half a block along Market Street. He asked about employment there, but they were not hiring.

He left the store, bought a newspaper, and walked to the Horn and Hardart Automat at Eighth and Chestnut for some pie and coffee. He spent over an hour reading the paper and looking in the want ads. There was a large box ad, "HELP WANTED, must have experience working with felts and leather, apply in person, John B. Stetson Hat Company, Germantown Avenue."

Peter's eyes lit up. Even with his failing memory, he knew this company and the building they were in. It was in a large building on Germantown Avenue. He walked by it many times, as it wasn't far from his store. He took the page with the ad and hopped on a northbound trolley. When Peter explained his experience processing goatskins, he was hired as an apprentice milliner. He was paid $50 a month, not enough for room and board, but he had a job and felt relieved.

Peter returned to the saloon and told James he found work, but not enough to rent a room and have enough for food and clothing. James said, "Look, Pete, you'll make enough to buy your food and clothes when you need something. You can use the cook kitchen here and stay in the back room as long as you want if you give the saloon a good clean'n early on Sunday mornings, all right?"

"Thanks, James, you are a good brother and always have been. You're the only one in the family that ever gave a damn about me. Thank you, brother. I'll have to go out today and buy a hat for the job."

"Why's that? Can't you buy one of their hats?"

"No, no, you have to come and go to work wearing a hat, but not a Stetson hat."

"Why's that?"

"Think about it." Peter paused and said, "They don't want ya steal'n their hats. Ya have to come and go from the building with a hat, but not a Stetson."

"Very clever, very smart of them; for sure, if not, every Irishman would look like a cowboy, and you too."

Peter laughed for the first time he could remember. He now had the schedule for his routine complete, mimicking that of his prison life, but it was life on the outside of the walls. He even bought a newspaper every Sunday and read it at the same time, ten o'clock to eleven o'clock, as he did in prison. His life was getting better. He also maintained his exercise regimen on a daily basis, doing push-ups and lifting beer kegs instead of his iron prison bed. This regular routine went on for the next eight and a half years.

CHAPTER 23

A Few Good Men
1910

I t was almost Christmas, 1910, when Peter went out for his usual
Saturday morning walk down Market Street toward the river, and
then he saw it; there was a different ship at the Chestnut Street
dock. It was a huge US Navy warship, and there were a lot of people
congregating at the dock. When he came closer, he saw the sign by
the gangway:

> OPEN HOUSE, USS *Warrington (DD-30)*
> Visitors Welcome
> US Navy and US Marine Corp
> Recruiting Centers at Bow and Stern
> Welcome Aboard

The USS *Warrington* was a Paulding-class destroyer built by
William Cramp and Sons, shipbuilders in Philadelphia. She was just
launched in June and was due to be commissioned the next spring.
The ship was on show to the public, at almost three hundred feet
long, and costing over $600,000, she was a sight to behold. It took
a year to build.[19]

The Warrington was not just for public view but for public
support of the US Navy and the Marine Corps.

---
[19] Wikipedia.

Twelve years before, the United States won the Spanish-American war, which started with the sinking of the battleship *Maine* in Havana harbor. The war was won, but the United States military continued to recruit forces needed well after the armistice and into the new century. The country still had a need for foreign oil and to be prepared for any further conflicts; the Spanish still had interests in the Caribbean, as well as in Central America, especially Venezuela and Nicaragua.[20] Peter walked up the gangway and toured the top deck. He had never seen anything like this. He was amazed. On the bow, under the two forward gun turrets, hung a canvas sign, "Ask about a Career in the Marines."

He approached a table where two Marine sergeants were sitting.

"Are you interested in a career with the Marines?"

"Well, I might be. What would I do if I signed up?"

"There are all sorts of MOSs to choose from. Here's the list."

Peter took the paper and scanned down the list entitled USMC MOS (Military Occupational Specialty). He came to number 30 on the list, "Supply, Administration, and Operations."

"Does anything there interest you?" said the recruiter.

"Well, number 30 looks interesting, yes, very interesting. Tell me more."

"Well, sir, that would be working for the quartermaster corps, but first, how old are you? You know, we are enlisting able men up to sixty years old."

"Well, I'm only fifty-eight," he lied.

"Really, you look no older than fifty, but before we go any further, we need to confirm your recent employment before we can talk about an enlistment and a MOS."

"Okay, I understand."

The first sergeant Peter spoke to said, "How's your health and physical fitness?" And with that, Peter unbuttoned his shirt and showed a flex of his biceps while taking a deep breath and striking the pose of a "muscleman." He looked two decades younger than he was.

---

[20] Ibid.

"Well, that's impressive for fifty-eight, I must say," the Marine said with a laugh. "You look great. Tell Sergeant York over there who you are and who your last two employers were."

Peter was in one of his more lucid moments, where everything was in focus. He said, "Well, right now, I am a milliner with the Stetson Hat Company, and before that, I was the owner of McNally and Son's Grocery at Eleventh and Master Streets till last year," he lied again.

The sergeant flipped through the pages of the "City Commercial Directory, 1890–1910." The sergeant said, "I don't find a Stetson Hat Company."

"Try looking under John J. Stetson," said Peter.

"All right, the directory shows Peter McNally, an employee of John J. Stetson Hat Company." Seeing it listed, the officer said, "When did you work at your grocery store?"

"A few years ago. Business was bad, so I shut it down," he lied again. "Sir, please proceed to the next desk. The officer will give you forms to fill out. After that, you will go below decks to deck two right through that open hatch and down the ladder. Be careful on the ladder now. You will be checked by a Marine corpsman for your fitness and general health, and then wait until we have ten recruits. You will all be sworn in as privates."

So by midday, Peter was a private in the United States Marine Corps.

When Peter was completing his enlistment papers, he mentioned that when the Civil War started, he enlisted and was in the inactive reserves. With that, the sergeant in charge said, "We will simply activate your reserve status. You should be recognized and commended for your previous service."

He received his orders to report to the US Marines Commandant at the Philadelphia Naval Shipyard in South Philadelphia the next morning at 0800 hours. He was given directions from the city center to take the Fifteenth Street trolley to the last stop and, from there, a few short walking directions to the front gate.

Peter told James of his decision to join the Marines and proudly showed him his orders.

Peter left the saloon just after James arrived the next morning. "Pete, I wish you luck. The job you just got by enlisting is a good one, plus you are serving your county, and the Marines will take good care of you. I wish you the best."

Peter was told he could bring some money but other than that, only the clothes on his back. He felt secure as he entered the gate of the base. He was processed, given his military uniforms and work clothes, and led to his barracks, a long building with a double row of twenty double-deck beds on each side with footlockers. He met his drill instructor and went through a very fast basic training regiment, taking only a week, after which, he was assigned to the Quartermaster Corp in building B-38.

His job was to help order supplies and food for the base. He just did as told, and the work suited him. The hours were only ten hours a day for five days a week. He worked in the base commissary on Saturdays; all the work was similar to what he did at the prison, so there was no stress.

The food on the base was good, much better, and healthier than prison food, and the daily military schedule mimicked that of the prison. He also got to meet many fine men.

He worked at the job for only a week. When at meals, he started getting a dull pain in his right jaw that got worse day by day, and soon, it was a sharp pain. The pain was accompanied by two quarter-sized open sores on his neck and jaw. They had been weeping for a week and wouldn't heal.

The first time he noticed any sensation in his jaw was in the shower on his last day at ESP, but that was over eight years ago, and nothing since then till now; he went to the medical center on the base and asked to see a corpsman.

After quite a wait, he finally went to an examining room, where a corpsman examined him. He looked at the weeping sores. He took swabs for examination under the microscope in the lab and also took an x-ray of his jaw.

Peter waited an hour and a half in the waiting room. Upon examining the swabs and x-rays, the corpsman told Peter the bad news, "Private, were you ever exposed to any toxic chemicals?"

Peter thought for a moment, "Well, yes, I worked in two tanneries some time ago, one in New York and one as a young man in Ireland."

"Well, I am sorry to tell you that you have a very rare form of cancer called sarcoma. It probably came from that exposure and took this long to show up. It's in your right jaw and neck, and unfortunately, there's no cure for it. The best we can do for you is to help you manage the pain and make you comfortable. We can give you a morphine drip for the pain. It will help you rest and sleep. I'm not sure how much time you will have. Do you have a priest you'd like to speak to or a relative?"

Peter was in shock. He couldn't believe at sixty-two, he was staring death in the face. "I don't have a priest but would like to speak with my brother, James." He gave the corpsman James's address.

Peter was placed in C Ward. It was on the first floor for convenience. C Ward was next to the morgue; all C Ward patients were terminal.

Peter was in C Ward for nine days. James came to visit and spent two hours talking. Both of the brothers cried uncontrollably. It was the third time in his life that Peter had ever cried. It was an emotional day.

The next day, Peter was not in touch with reality. That night and for the next four nights, there was a full moon, the large, reddish-orange moon that haunted Peter all his life, a Devil Moon. For the next few days, it continued its haunting, shining into the C Ward window onto Peter's face as he slept.

On the fourth night in C Ward, in the middle of the night, while Peter slept, the moonlight streamed through the ward window and the glass drip chamber of the morphine bottle suspended by Peter's bed; the light from the bottle took on the color of the moon and painted a spectrum of color over Peter's face as he slept.

The next afternoon, the day nurse came for an afternoon visit. "Is there anything I can get for you, private, to make you more comfortable?"

Peter was awake and heard the question and, after a long pause, said in an almost inaudible voice, "Yes, yes…Katie, I need to see my baby, Katie." His eyes were filled with tears. It was only the fourth time in his life he had cried.

"Where's your baby, private? Where's Katie? Where can I find her? Who is she with?" the nurse asked.

Peter mumbled something else under his breath that she couldn't understand. The nurse leaned down toward him to hear. "What is it, private?"

Peter closed his tear-filled eyes, and the nurse heard him whisper, "God, forgive me." He slipped away into eternity at 4:10 in the afternoon on the 20th of January 1910. Peter was dead and free at last.

Five miles to the north, in the Irish Gray's Ferry section of South Philadelphia, Edward was getting ready to go shopping at Wanamaker's for the new boots he wanted for Christmas but didn't get, while Bridget and her granddaughter, Rose Genevieve, were busy making an apple pie.

CHAPTER 24

January 1910
Dust to Dust

On January 22, at 0500 hours, the bugle sounded at the Philadelphia Navy Base. Reveille brought the day to life at the base.

If the weather had been fair, the sun would have been rising soon and the sky brightening, but on this day, the sky was dark, unusually dark, and remained dark all day. It was a sullen sunless sky day. In stark contrast, there were small silvery snowflakes gently drifting to the ground from a windless sky.

The six marines assigned to Peter's burial ceremony finished their breakfast mess, returned to their quarters, and put on their dress uniforms for Peter's funeral and interment.

As requested, James McNally came to the main gate at 0900, where he was directed and met the funeral procession, a new Marine motorized hearse, and two staff cars.

James, now an old man at eighty-four, was the only family member present because he was the only family member notified. James, along with the base chaplain and the other marines, took the slow ten-mile drive through slush-covered streets westward to Yeadon, where Peter was interned in the Navy 1 section of Mt. Moriah Cemetery. The cemetery straddled the Philadelphia boundary line with Yeadon in Delaware County.

The small funeral cortege proceeded slowly through the large center arch of the massive brownstone entranceway, which had castle-like towers on each side, each topped with typical castle tower-like crenelations; it made for a rather dramatic entrance experience into the cemetery.

There were no other visitors except the grave-digging crew waiting in the distance to cover the grave. The air was cold and crisp, and, except for the crunch of the Marine party's shoes on the snow cover, it was dead silent.

Light snow was still falling as six marines, in a slow, shuffling march, carried Peter's flag-draped coffin from the hearse to the gravesite.

The burial service was short. The Marine chaplain said a prayer at the graveside as the six marines stood at attention, three on each side of the flag-draped casket.

The chaplain expounded, "With the certain hope of the resurrection to eternal life, through our Lord Jesus Christ, we commend to Almighty God our brother in service, Private Peter David McNally. We hereby commit his body to this resting place, earth to earth, ashes to ashes, dust to dust. May the Lord bless him and keep him. May the Lord make his face shine upon him and be gracious to him. May the Lord lift up his countenance upon him and give him peace. Amen."

The marines folded the flag into a triangle as it was being removed and presented it to James. The bugler played taps. The chaplain and marines returned to their vehicles and drove back to the base.

That day, the sun did not shine when it rose in the sky, nor did it shine all day, and into the night, the waning moon did not shine. It was a day and night of unordinary darkness.

USMC Private Peter David McNally's grave is marked with an engraved marble headstone. The original headstone had deteriorated. Volunteers working for the Navy replaced the gravestone in 2016. The grave is in the Navy 1 section of the cemetery, sixth from the east line, thirteenth from the south line, in the Yeadon, Delaware County, a section of St. Mariah Cemetery.

Only one person ever visited Peter's grave, and that was one hundred eleven years after his burial; that person is his great-grandson, this author.

FINIS

Ashes to ashes, dust to dust

EPILOGUE

Alia McLeod, 1794
Glasgow, Scotland

Catherine Ann's friend (a fictional character) was "tried" by the church elders and sent to an asylum for unwed mothers just south of Glasgow, where she gave birth to a daughter she named Hope. When Hope was one year old, she was sent to an orphanage. Alia never saw her daughter again and lived out her life there, working in the asylum laundry.

"The asylums were refuges for the 'Fallen women of Scotland' in the eighteenth and nineteenth centuries. Prostitutes, single mothers, and even socialists were admitted to the Magdalene Asylums to be trained in the habits of industry and sobriety. At its height, the organization, which operated around the world, had twenty such refuges in Scotland. It was two hundred years before the abuses were discovered through an investigation."[21]

Hope McLeod, Alia's illegitimate baby daughter, was sent to an orphanage just south of Glasgow at one year old. She, along with other children, was physically and sexually abused. One night, because she was crying loudly, a nun beat her to death with a cane. A "Devil Moon" rose over the orphanage that night. This character is fictional, and her killing is fictional, but based on what was typical in that place at that time; an expose article exposed the

---

[21] The Scotsman News, Internet.

186

dastardly acts in The Scotsman, News, which was posted on the internet:

> By 1858, there were eight such homes for orphans
> and the elderly run by "The Little Sisters of the
> Poor," also known as "The Sisters of Nazarene."

The investigations found numerous unmarked graves of children on the grounds of the orphanages.

This lunacy-abuse and killing carried well into the twentieth century at these homes around the world.

Mary McNally left the family at age twenty-three. Everyone except her mother considered her the black sheep of the family. She never developed a strong relationship with either of her parents or siblings but did correspond with her mother. She eventually moved from New York to South Philadelphia, away from the rest of the family. She married and had six children.

Agnes McNally Kelly continued to work in the bakery with her husband, John, and their son, James. She also continued with her dressmaking business. Agnes did volunteer work with St. Malachy's Church for the remainder of her years.

Catherine "Kate" Ann McNally—Several years after Catherine's death, her will was probated. She gifted $25,000 to Catholic charities.

Joseph McNally started a painting business in South Philadelphia after leaving the family store. He lived with his wife Nora and died from natural causes in 1944. He never bothered to seek out or contact any of his living relatives. He and Nora never had any children.

Sarah Cunningham—After Peter's trial, Sarah was getting less and less active due to her age. Her usual friends were either dead, didn't keep up contact, or had moved.

Her daughter Bridget and her grandchildren decided it would be best if she lived in an old-age home associated with St. Malachy's Roman Catholic Church.

The facility where Sarah moved was in the twelfth ward on Church Street. She liked it there. She made many friends quickly, and her last days were pleasant with the one hundred other women residents. She died of natural causes just short of her ninetieth birthday in 1922.

Bridget Cunningham McNally, Peter's wife, at age sixty-six, moved when the store closed. She, along with Edward and PJ, rented a house at 1275 Bucknell Street in the Grays Ferry area of South Philadelphia, an Irish neighborhood. They all went to St. Gabriel's church a few blocks away.

In 1915, Bridget, at the age of eighty-one, died from myocarditis, complications of an inflamed heart muscle. She and the other family members, except for Peter's half-brother, never heard of Peter's actual whereabouts or death.

James Cunningham McNally, Peter's half-brother, continued to own and operate "McPherson's Saloon" until his death in 1916. He died in his sleep when he was eighty-six. In his later years, he often had visits from his niece Agnes. Neither ever spoke about the family tragedy. Families didn't dig into the past in those days, especially when the past involved the murder of a family member by a family member.

James McNally, Peter's son, lived at #51 on the east side of South Sixth Street by himself, a bachelor, and other than some brief time working at the family store, he only had one job in Philadelphia, as a laborer at the Baldwin Locomotive Works. He hung around with a rough crowd and was always getting into fights. He died suddenly on December 8, 1897, at the age of thirty-one. No autopsy was done, but it was thought it may have been a brain hemorrhage.

Six years before, when he was twenty-five, he was involved in a major altercation and was hit on the head with a brick. The fight made the newspapers; that incident could have caused an aneurysm that was just waiting to burst.

He was buried in the family plot at New Cathedral Cemetery. James was loved by his mother but not by any of the others. The feelings were mutual, with the exception of his uncle James, who closed his saloon for the day to attend his nephew's funeral and burial.

PJ, Peter Joseph McNally, met Edna Mays, a protestant and farmer's daughter from Lancaster County, in 1902. When they met, she was at the Reading Terminal Market with her father, bringing in produce for sale.

After courting for about six months, they got married and moved to #21 Emily Street in South Philadelphia. When he met Edna, he told her his name was Joseph Peter. He changed his name, not legally, but because he did not want to have any possible connection to his father, even though the murder was ten years before. PJ kept the family secret, even from Edna, never revealing much information about his father. When asked about his parents, aunts, uncles, or siblings, it was always, "Oh, they're all gone now." PJ died in 1958 from a complication of Alzheimer's disease.

PJ was this author's grandfather.

Peter's father, Daniel David McNally, and his half-brother Charles James McNally moved to Glasgow, Scotland, in 1865. Charles became an experienced spirits merchant in Dublin, but the famine had such a toll on his lower-class customers that he knew he had to leave Dublin; he moved with his father, Daniel, to Glasgow.

Three years later, after opening a spirit shop on Matheson Street in Glasgow, Charles met a young man, Andrew Dewar Rattray, in 1868. Andrew had just started a business on Kirkoswald Street that blended whiskeys and retailed the scotch whiskey blend. They became best of friends...the beginning of Dewars White Label, a blended scotch whiskey. Daniel David McNally, Peter's father, died on January 21, 1873, in Glasgow at the age of sixty-five from peritonitis, a bacterial disease of the abdomen; there were no antibiotics at the time to save him.

Charles James McNally—After his father's death, Charles lived alone and continued the spirits business in Glasgow, Scotland. He died in 1892 at the ripe old age of eighty-nine from natural causes. The doctor said he either died from tipping more than a few wee drams of Dewar's whiskey every day, his favorite, or he lived that long because of his imbibing; the doctor hinted the latter was probably the case.

Edward McNally lived in the Grays Ferry area of south Philadelphia with his mother, Bridget, and PJ, Peter Joseph, his brother, who lived with them for a short time. Edward eventually married and had a child named Rose Genevieve. Edward died in 1940 at the age of seventy-eight.

James Kelly, Peter D. McNally's grandson, was the only witness to the shooting of his aunt Kate. He worked in his parents' bakery with his mother and father until he was eighteen, and then moved to south Philadelphia with his grandmother and his uncles Edward, and PJ.

The whereabouts of James and any details of his adult life are unknown.

USS *Battleship Maine*—years after the sinking, in a post-mortem war investigation, it came to be known that the sinking was, in fact, an accident. It was learned that munitions exploded because they were stored too close to the boilers. Because it was our government's mistake, not much was ever reported in the papers or on the news.

The Devil Moon—since the dawn of time, when the first man looked into the night sky, the moon was always fascinating and sometimes captivating. Our moon has never changed; however, it still often casts its spell of lunacy on some unsuspecting souls.

The Skeleton in the Closet—the skeleton in this true story was revealed after being a family secret for 123 years, and if not for my curiosity about my paternal family on ancestry.com, it would never have been found.

AUTHOR'S
AFTERWORD

A Devil Moon followed my family, especially my great-grandfather. Was he really subject to its spell? Who knows? He was a good, hardworking man with the best intentions for his family, but seemingly, he was overcome by the powers of darkness that led to bouts of depression and periods of temporary insanity. The depression was compounded by business failures, the deaths of children, along with the toxic effects on his body from breathing the chemical fumes of tanneries in his early years. During his life, he experienced times of dementia and what during those times was known as lunacy, which actually may have been undiagnosed Alzheimer's disease.

Although I never knew my great-grandfather, Peter David, while I was growing up, I knew his son, my grandfather, Peter Joseph (PJ in the book), and his wife, Edna Mayes McNally, who lived three doors from our house on the street behind us. As a kid, I visited with them regularly. My grandmother Edna was a dressmaker and seamstress; in fact, she taught me how to sew. She also had a severe dislike for what she called the "Papes." PJ was one of the last Catholics on my branch of the McNally family tree. Edna saw to that.

My father, Joseph Edward McNally, was born in 1903. He was named after his two uncles. My grandfather obviously looked up to them. He never met his grandfather, Peter David, who, at the time my father was born, was still living in Eastern State Penitentiary and then with his stepbrother James. My father also likely never knew about the murder of his Aunt Kate, nor did Edna. There would be no good reason for PJ to tell anyone of this horrible part of the family history.

I seriously doubt my father ever met any of his relatives, as he never once mentioned one by name. In many ways, I was closer to my grandfather than my father. PJ retired in the early 1940s from the printing plant where he worked beside my father, who ran a letterpress, and who also started work at the age of fourteen after attending only one day in high school.

After retirement, my grandfather did handyman work at the homes of Edna's wealthy clients. He was good with hand tools and taught me how to use them, a skill that was passed down through the generations. He showed me how to sharpen a handsaw and the proper way to hold a hammer. Since Edna worked full-time, "Grand-pop," as I called him, did all the cooking. He taught me how to cook. Breakfast was his favorite meal, and his favorite menu was waffles, fried eggs with lots of pepper, toast, coffee, and freshly squeezed orange juice (it didn't come any other way back then). This is still a favorite breakfast of mine, including lots of pepper.

Grand-pop always had a good-sized vegetable garden in his backyard, and each year, he gave me seeds and a corner of the garden to grow them. He taught me how to thin them out, weed, water, and care for them. I still love gardening.

He didn't talk that much because Edna was so domineering. My father was the same way. I remember the time I asked Grand-pop if he had any brothers and sisters. "They're all gone now" is all he ever said. Other than that, his father owned a grocery store.

What a surprise when I found through my research on Ancestry that my grandfather was one of seven children who lived to adulthood.

That revelation sent me deeper into researching my family. I was not very good at navigating Ancestry, but with help from my cousin's wife, Carole Reeves, I found my great-grandfather in the 1900 census. He was residing with fifty other men listed on the census sheet. I scrolled up to find this was but one sheet of the census sheets at Eastern State Penitentiary. But how he got there, I had to find out.

I subscribed to NewspaperArchives.com and bracketed the years 1890 to 1900. I entered Peter D. McNally, Philadelphia newspapers, and keyword "Prison"…bingo! There it was, front-page news on the

Philadelphia Inquirer, October 15, 1893, "SHOT DOWN BY HER OWN FATHER—Peter McNally shot his daughter Kate in her grocery store."

NewspaperArchives.com provided digital copies of actual news articles about the murder and full coverage of Peter's trial.

Besides ancestry.com, I found more information on irishheritage.com and familysearch.com. Some of this information overlapped, often with conflicting names and dates as to births and deaths. I chose to use the names that appeared the most and that were more consistent, and I used the dates that best fit the story and aligned better with more recent records on Ancestry or facts that were reported in the Philadelphia newspapers.

My apologies to any of my distant relatives for possible errors that may have occurred while researching our family history.

The last bit of research I conducted was to visit the New Cathedral Cemetery in north Philadelphia, where most of the family were buried, and to visit St Moriah Cemetery in Yeadon, Pennsylvania, to visit Peter's grave. While the location of the graves at New Cathedral Cemetery was on the cemetery map, there were no markers or tombstones. They likely deteriorated over the years, as there were no grave markers of that vintage in the cemetery.

The St. Moriah Cemetery is the largest military cemetery in Pennsylvania, including a ten-acre Navy plot. Peter's original tombstone was replaced by the current one by the Veterans Administration National Cemetery Association in 2020, ironically, the same year I started writing this book.

Since researching my great-grandfather's life with the tragedies of the deaths of his children, I feel very blessed that somehow I made it here, and beyond that, I'm very happy that I decided to write this book, Peter's story and the story of how the McNally family came to America. I hope you enjoyed reading it.

ACKNOWLEDGMENTS

A special thank you to my cousin by marriage, Barbara Reeves, for her hours of work, persistence, dedication, and encouragement. The book would not have happened without her. Thank you, Barbara.

The idea of a book was spawned with help from another cousin by marriage, Carole Reeves, who assisted me in searching ancestry.com. Together, we found the skeleton in the closet. Thank you, Carole.

The author's photograph on the back cover is by Michael D. Roe, the author's grandson, who lives in Naples, Florida. Thank you, Michael.

Thanks to Annie Anderson, a researcher at Eastern State Penitentiary, for Peter's mug shots and Peter's prison history.

The front and back cover designs were a collaboration between the author and Palmyra, New Jersey, artist, and illustrator Ulana Zahajkewycz, who provided the graphic and artistic interpretations of the author's ideas. Thank you, Ulana.

A special thank you to my friend Margaret Mary Gestaut for her invaluable help with the final edits.

Thank you to Rachel Nicely, my publishing assistant at Fulton books, for her constant availability, assistance, and encouragement.

Author's contact: MBrownMcNally.com
info@MBrownMcNally.com

Printed in the USA
CPSIA information can be obtained
at www.ICGtesting.com
LVHW061044170823
755275LV00002B/266